TO LOVE A VAMPIRE

To Love a Vampire

USA TODAY BESTSELLING AUTHOR
A.K. KOONCE

To Love a Vampire

Cover design by Killer Book Covers

Editing by Proofreading by the Page

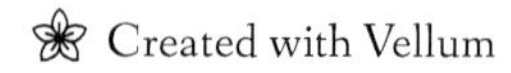

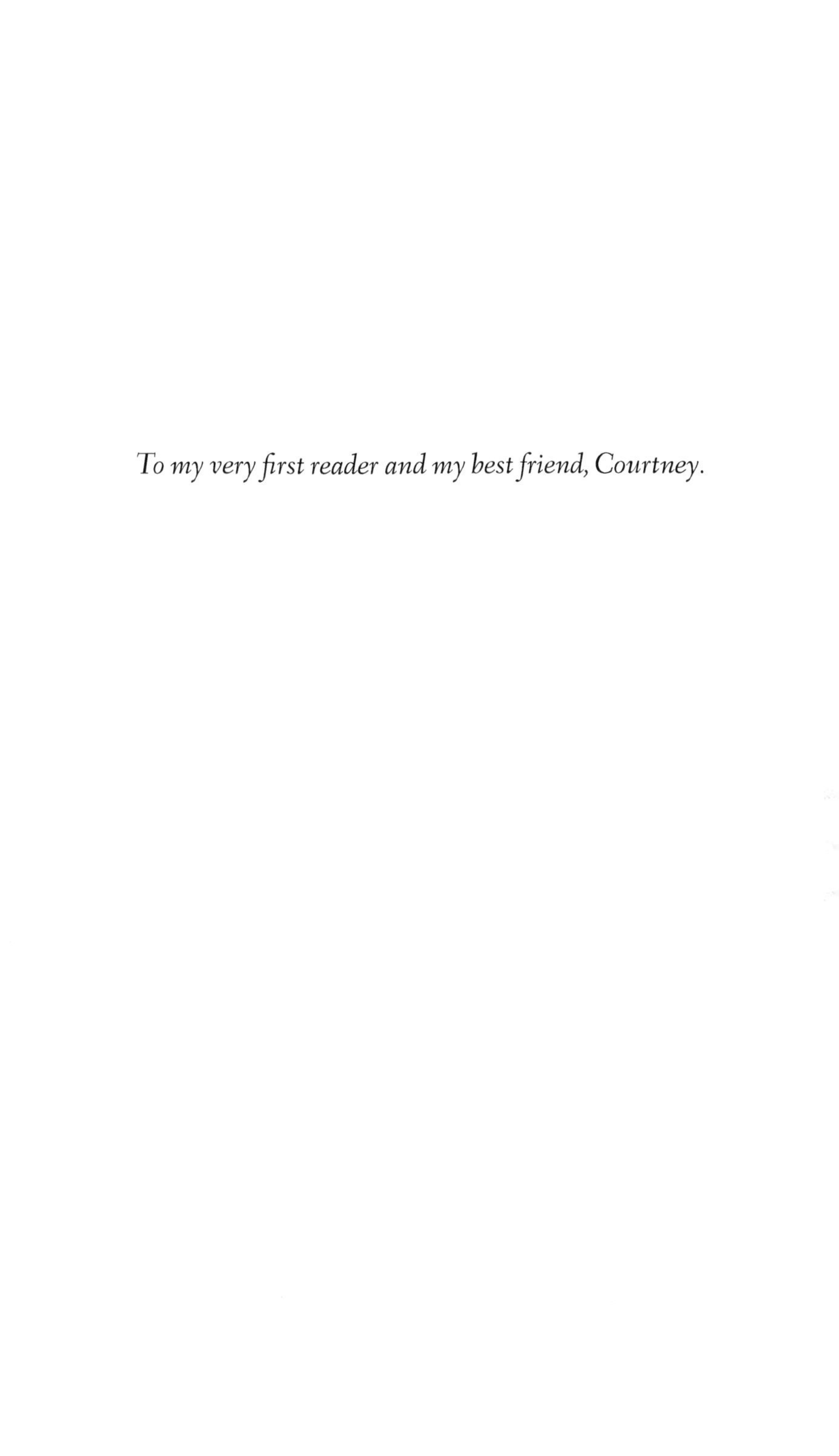

To my very first reader and my best friend, Courtney.

CONTENTS

ONE
A SECRET SOCIETY

My knees drop into the thick mud, sinking me closer into the bay water that my mother's bloody and disfigured remains drifted out into all those months ago. The Emerald Ocean took her away from me on calm waters. A shuddering breath pushes past dry lips. My usually closed emotions come tumbling out of the door as soon as it cracks open.

It's late. The normally clear water is a mass of inky black waves, hinting at the mystical creatures that lurk beneath the serene surface. The moon is nothing more than a sliver of color slashed across the dark sky. Minimal light scatters into the shadowy surroundings.

All my life, I had never seen a real mystic, but now, I know they've always been here. They've carefully hidden themselves away from the mortals, watching us from afar.

The unseen fae of the Emerald Ocean are a perfect example. Anyone could happen upon the beautiful water source, I've come here hundreds of times now, and yet, I've never once seen what lies on the other side of the eerie water. The world below the surface is a hidden cove, tucked quietly away from society. This sort of separation seems to work for the mortals and the mystics.

For now.

The world slips away from me in this moment, though. Closing my eyes, I force the surrounding noise from my head. Leaves begin to quiet in the wind, the restless owl in the tree is now unheard, the distant beating of drums dissolves until only my pounding heart is heard in its place. Reality silences to find a few moments of peace in my muddled mind.

Inhaling the cool night air, I can almost smell all those evenings we spent by the crackling fire. The memory of his silver gaze always sparkles within the starry sky. His smile is unclear in my memory, never quite right, but his beautifully sad eyes are always perfect.

I can't remember how my mother's voice sounded and that alone is enough to make me want to scream, my chest growing tight and constricted. It just isn't fair. There are so many things I should have said to her. Unspoken and repentant filled words slice like broken glass through my thoughts.

The love and tragedy they left me with are always there, carried around with me every day, just under the deep layer of pain in my chest.

Behind me, a twig snaps in the forest and my hand

instantly slides over the smooth hilt of the sword at my hip. *His sword.* Another thing he left me with, another reminder to physically carry around. I open my eyes but remain motionless. My sight is no longer watching and dreaming of the stars up above but is now searching the darkness for the source of the noise.

"Are you coming tonight, Princess?" a deep and sulking voice calls out to me.

I release the breath I was holding hostage within my lungs and let go of the hilt of the sword. It's just Kaino. My eyes burn with unshed tears, all the unshed tears I've refused to release for months. Strangely my body feels stronger with the tension pressing in on my chest.

Next month will be one year. But it doesn't matter. A day. A year. A lifetime. I'll never see my mother or Asher or even Ky, again. The hole in my heart shudders but doesn't quite close.

A slow sigh releases from my heavy lungs and I give myself one more second.

With reluctance, I stand. Thick mud and debris covers my jeans and boots. A sloshing sound accompanies my steps from the bay to the dry land where Kaino's dark, animalistic eyes greet me. He's taller than me by a few inches but something within him cringes away from me. Not physically, but I'm left at arm's length no matter how much his father forces us together.

White tendrils of smoke waft into the night sky behind him, an unseen fire accompanies the beat of the drum deep within the woods.

"I didn't think you'd join us tonight," he drawls in a bored, even tone. His eyes pause on the glowing Crimson Sword, before taking my arm in his. Everyone here is careful not to touch the mystical blade that never leaves my hip.

We walk through the forest, the dry leaves crunching beneath our boots. The smell of burning wood sails through the cool night air.

Kaino's hard eyes never stop scanning the shadows. He's a mystic of few words and even fewer emotions but a mind that seems to never sleep. His posture is stiff, much like that of the other warriors of the Wandering lands, but his is different. Distant, like he'd rather not be arm and arm with me—or anyone for that matter. As if my touch might set him on fire. He's never given me the feeling he doesn't like me. In fact, he's one of the few friends I have here.

My life in the Wandering community is the total opposite of my life in the work camp. My friends and family are gone, along with the controlled lifestyle I once lived. The government doesn't interfere with the Wanderers like they do the human camps. Part of me thinks the hidden society of mystics is a threat to the humans. It would explain the secret treaty between this community and the government.

I'm the only human here. It's odd; last year I had never met a mystic and now they accept me as one of their own.

I was lucky to be brought here. To find such a safe

haven within the hell I have lived. It's a miraculous feeling to feel safe and alive when you once felt death rattling your slow beating heart.

The Wanderers are something different, something unique in today's restrained world. They are *free*. They are encouraged to live how they please, to grow old however they like. As long as they remain a secret society the government will never hinder their way of life. Only if they do not interfere with the controlled villages south of here. The villages I once lived in. The friends I left behind are still forced to work and live and even reproduce how the government directs them.

I shake the weighted thought from my mind before it manifests into anything more.

In the darkness, I peer at my friend as we walk through the thick forest. Kaino is a friend but never revealing. Never personal. I know as much about Kaino as his exterior allows me and he, in return, knows the same about myself.

He's actually quite handsome. Giving him another side glance, my eyes trail dark brooding features, which are embellished even more when his long lashes brush against high cheek bones. He could be more handsome, if he wasn't so stern all the time; a frown eternally etched across his face.

I was offered one of his secrets when we first met. Only one in the entire year that I've been here. Just under the bulky muscle of the warrior's scarred body, lies a dormant trait. A trait that the Wanderers have kept sheathed for nearly a decade in cooperation with The Exception Treaty.

Beneath Kaino's detached expressions and his depthless dark eyes, lies an animal rattling its cage to get out. An animal that's kept caged in honor of the treaty between the Wanderers and the government. An animal that might be consuming Kaino from the inside out.

A werewolf.

Kaino leads us toward the raging flames in the distance. The flickering fire is held high by strong logs twice my size and make the mystics seem small and insignificant, despite their dominant personalities. Laughter and music blow through the breeze the closer we come to the gathering. Tonight's celebration is the biggest I have seen.

He leans in close to me and whispers in a deep voice, his warm breath fanning my cheek, "I'm glad you chose to join us. Every Wanderer will be present for tonight's celebration."

I nod at his words, my eyes scanning the crowd. The Wanderers *celebrate* every night. In their culture, every day is a celebration because their people didn't always have the freedoms they have now. So rejoice, drink, love, and repeat.

It's true though, it is an enormous turnout. Hundreds of people are gathered in the clearing before us. I watch as females in minimal clothing dance barefoot on the dry dusty ground. Some of the males in their usual attire, shirtless with black jeans and black boots, drink and laugh while others sway with the females to the pounding drums. The structure of their bodies are finely lined with a lifetime of training and strength. The werewolves are fearless to the point of carelessness, a confidence flows off of them with every breath they take.

Their clothes are usually what gives their heritage away. The warriors and wolves who make up most of the Wandering community refuse to wear anything constricting. They'd probably be naked if they could; their feral instincts just pushing at the surface to get out. The fae, though there are few within the village, are easily recognized by their beauty as well as their formal, crisp attire. Intelligence and mischievousness dances within their always watchful eyes.

As a human, I try my best to just blend in. My main goal is to truly go unnoticed. Not that that method works for me, the village *princess*. I struggle to keep the disgust from my face every time I hear the mocking title.

A single Infinity witch also mars this culture. She fills me with pain every time my gaze meets her pale green eyes that are identical to my own. My stomach twists, the breath dying on my lips... She's the ghosting image of my mother.

Asher once told me Infinity witches appear as we wish them to. Their features are made up of our desires and hopes. It pains me that my hope is to see my mother, I can't even look at her without tears burning my eyes. I spot her white blond hair instantly in the crowd and bite my lip until I taste blood, blinking hard until my eyes focus on anything else. With my focus kept on the blazing fire, I can still feel her eerie presence even as the flames scorch my sight.

Does she know what I see?

"Two weeks until our annual Treaty Celebration. Representatives from the city will join us in honor of our years of friendship. We celebrate to honor them as our guests. So tonight, we must revel even more for the lack of fun we will have in the preparing weeks," Kaino says through clenched teeth.

He chances a glance at me out of the corner of his eye and I pretend to keep my focus on the flickering fire. He looks away quickly, taking a cup of alcohol off the closest table as we walk into the heart of the party. The warmth of the flames and the crowd floods my body.

People sway and dance around us. A few wolves watch me closely as I suppress the anger and annoyance that threatens to bubble to the surface, allowing it to smother out in my constricted breaths instead. Their eyes ignore the set of my jaw, the way my fists clench at my sides, the rigid posture of my shoulders and spine. They ignore the way they make me feel—just seeing an object.

Since the Wanderer's leader, Lord Raske, first told me of his idea to join our races, to submissively put pressure on our government—to put a stop to the segregation within our society— every male I pass seems to think I'm a plaything. Something to be won in honor of their *lord.*

The idea of a human joining with one of the minority races to end the decades of segregation, abuse and imprisonment is laughable. It would take more than one happy union to make a dent in our country's oppression.

"Have any of them found the nerve to talk to the intimidating human girl yet?" someone asks over my shoulder.

Turning toward the voice, my lips tug into a half smile at Luca as she hands me a drink. She's tall with unnatural maroon hair that's shaved on one side. Confidence and strength radiates from her with every move she makes. A slash of beauty spreads over her face as she smiles back at me, revealing perfect white teeth. Teeth that are entirely...

Predator like.

A prowling stealth guides her steps, eyes sweeping in every detail of her surroundings. A carefully poised aggression sheathed beneath a soft and beautiful exterior.

She was my savior when Shaw's men attacked. My stomach falls at the memory of my near death and the deaths of those who I love. I push the thought down into the darkness of my mind. "Not yet, but I'm sure they're just waiting for our Prince to let his guard down," I say, throwing a glance at Kaino, who stands with perfect posture at my side.

"Like these mystics would know what to say to anyone as beautiful as you." Kaino doesn't look at me as he speaks, keeping his eyes on the festivities, all but ignoring me. His half compliment is masked by a blank and careless expression.

A captivating water fae named Nerissa saunters by us. She brushes her curvy frame against Kaino's bulking arm, sending him a welcoming smile that touches her emerald eyes, eyes that are as deep as the ocean... the ocean that she crawled right out of. A cringe scurries through his immense body, his spine becoming like steel as he pulls away from her touch, a glare hardening his hooded features. The title he holds as commander is washed away, a shrinking figure left hunched in his place.

Her wispy long green hair disappears into the crowd; she doesn't give the scowling commander a second look.

Kaino's strange but kind words circle my mind again and I can't help but smile into my drink. The smirk causes a pain to flare in my stomach, so I bite my lip and the happiness is pulled away as quickly as it came. "Careful. That was nearly a compliment," I warn before taking a big drink. The alcohol burns and threatens to take my breath away but I'm so familiar with the sensation the drink brings, that I no longer feel the effects of it when it passes over my tongue and down my throat.

An empty expression fills his dark eyes, his emotions once again lost within his calculating mind.

"Only an observation, Princess."

Luca rolls her eyes and pushes Kaino away. His stumbling steps shuffle a bit under the unnatural power she holds. A look passes between the two of them, a smirking and playful moment, before Kaino walks off toward a group of other warriors and doesn't look back at us in the shadows of the firelight.

What many within our community don't know – another blanketed secret– is Kaino and Luca are brother and sister—half brother and sister. Unlike the village I grew up in, many people here have half and step siblings. The community is very open minded. Something I am still adjusting to.

Luca takes my arm and leads me to get another drink. Unlike Kaino, Luca really is my friend. My only friend. She knows everything. Everything I had. Everything I lost. Everything I now am. She found me alone and dying and made the two days hike back to the Wanderers. A place that accepts the broken and tries to find pieces to put you back together again. Though, I am still standing, I still have tears and scars that the Wanderers will never fix.

I remember the tree we passed when I first arrived. I was starving and bleeding out. Luca dragged me the whole way. I thought I'd die before the graceful warrior got me to wherever she was taking me. But, I remember the tree like it was the gate to heaven. At the time, I had no idea what to make of my saviors.

Carved into the rough bark of the largest redwood I'd ever seen, were the jagged words *Wanderers Welcome*. The words sunk into me, filling my gentle heartbeats and broken limbs with a strange feeling. A feeling of hope.

"Ahhh and so the circus begins." A wolfish smile slashes across Luca's face.

As someone approaches, I turn with another drink already in my hand. I brace myself for whatever wolf might be lurking, but to my surprise it isn't a wolf at all.

"Hello, Declan." I give a short, careless nod, refusing to fully acknowledge the hybrid.

"Hello, Fallon." He gives a mocking nod in return.

Declan is an outcast among castaways. The confident hybrid-vampire moves to stand next to me, earning himself scowls from a few nearby warriors, their rivaling wolf instincts simmering just under the surface. Clearly, he also wants to watch those who watch me... and maybe piss them off in the process.

His calm and familiar presence is enough for fire to burn through me. Something similar to anger and hate settles around my fingertips, and I have to clench my fist at my side to keep the placid look on my face.

I don't hate him, I have no reason to. And yet, the reminder his features bring is enough to build unwarranted fury within me.

"I haven't missed the first yet, have I?" he asks, playing with a lock of my long brown hair that Luca had twisted and weaved into a beautiful cascading masterpiece this morning.

I swat his hand away lightly and take a step back from him, my spine tensing with every move. He reminds me too much of someone else but also not at all. He's tall and blonde with the steely eyes of his kind. I haven't been able to look him in the eye since we met. He knows he makes me uncomfortable but he has no idea why. Annoyingly, my distance seems to only cause more of a fascination within him.

"Some might say you're the first, Declan," Luca says, scanning the crowd like a hungry cat in a field of mice.

Declan assesses every inch of my body, his eyes burning over my skin. The clothes I wear are similar to the other females but much less revealing. Luca chooses to wear thin, black material that wraps around her chest and ties in the back with matching material around her waist that falls to her mid-thigh. No one sweats much in the Wandering community because no one wears much clothing, an enticing choice of fashion that only seems to breed their lax perspective of love.

It took me months to adjust from the modest clothes of the village I left behind and my fingers still fidget at my bare shoulders and the few inches of my exposed torso, itching to hide my insecurities as much as possible.

"Why are your jeans muddy? Why are you even wearing jeans?" Declan asks like it's the most urgent issue we might ever have. He glares at the tight jeans that cover my legs, the dry dirt that crusts my boots, and follows the length of my body up to the crossing black top that ties around my neck.

The jagged scar along my rib cage that's barely peeking out tingles against the cool night air and I force my hands not to show weakness at acknowledging the imperfection and memory.

"Why are *you* wearing jeans, Declan?" I ask in a childish tone, taking a sip of the warm alcohol.

Okay, not my best response.

His smile lights up his eyes like I just correctly answered his question. He leans in close and I can feel him brush against my thick, curly hair. "I'd happily take them off if you wished, love," he says in a hushed whisper that runs down my neck.

I roll my eyes and clench my jaw as I swing my elbow back into his stomach. I hit hard. Hard enough to hurt me as well as him—probably myself more than him. Slowly, he puts one arm over his stomach protectively and laughs. His calm and quiet laughter is almost enough to make me murder him on the spot. His happiness feels so genuine it almost physically hurts me, my chest heaving tight as I realize it's an emotion that no longer exists for me.

Luca shifts towards us in a defensive stance but I shake my head at her as Declan stalks away.

"I'm surprised they haven't thrown the hybrid out yet."

Guilt smothers me as Luca's statement sinks in. She's right, Declan isn't accepted even within the mystic community...

An hour passes with incredible slowness. I'm content listening to Luca describe a new defensive training technique that she's been working with me on when someone lingers into our conversation.

"I could always join you ladies tomorrow to show you firsthand how that's actually done," a tall and stocky warrior says with a smile. His height towers over me but as Luca pushes her shoulders back, I realize she meets him at eye level. "It's one thing to talk through or mimic these skills but it helps to have training with someone who has had experience in battle." That charming smile is still spread wide as he leans into me. Clearly, he has no idea what he just said.

Stalking with careful intent, Luca moves past me, brushing my arm against hers, a predatory swagger in her stride. Her glowering eyes hold his until she's toe to toe with the warrior. Slender bare feet brush the tips of his shining black boots. She harnesses his cautious but curious stare and her revealing and pretty outfit exposes the toned muscles in her back, arms, legs, and stomach.

"If you don't turn away from our conversation that you rudely interrupted, *right now,*" her eyes shine against the fire behind him, her words slow and meaningful, "you'll have even more experience on the receiving end of that particular technique to brag about."

His head tilts slightly, calculatingly, dark mahogany eyes question the ability of the beautiful female standing before him. The once pleasant smile is washed from his face as he bares his teeth. A spasm shakes his jaw, threatening to reveal the beast beneath the surface.

A few fae nearby stop dancing to the rhythm of the drum and watch the three of us, their interest spiking through the tension around me. Waiting. Two warlocks drinking next to us glance our way but continue their conversation without missing a beat.

The warrior takes one last look into Luca's menacing eyes before brushing past her, his shoulder knocking against hers. He walks far into the large crowd and doesn't look back.

I take another sip of my warm drink, letting it set uncomfortably in my stomach, as Luca stares into the distance where the warrior disappeared.

"I'm not trying to brag, but me taking my pants off would have been more entertaining than that, I promise," Declan whispers to me as he leisurely walks by.

The tension leaves my body in an instant. I close my eyes and force the smile from touching my solemn lips.

TWO
REJECTION

THE NIGHT IS PASSING with little entertainment. It's nearly two in the morning and the Wanderers show no sign of slowing down the party. Their normally swift feet stumble against the dry dirt, their movements more and more staggering as the night carries on. Luca caught the attention of an abnormally handsome fae over an hour ago and has been dancing the night away.

Entering the large military style tent feels like a bad choice but I walk inside anyway. The question I've been set on asking for the past few months has been burning inside me and consuming my thoughts. Taking a deep breath, I hold courage in my lungs to ask what I've already asked nearly half a dozen times now.

The layers of the thick tan fabric that creates four walls of the tent shield the air flow but it's not uncomfortably hot. Unless you're nervous and have had a little too much to drink.

I swallow hard and wipe the sweat from my palms on my dark jeans, pieces of dried mud flake off against my fingertips, momentarily distracting me as I grind the pebbles of dirt into dust. My heart pounds loudly, flushing my face with heat as I try to recall the words I want to say.

A few mystics lean against a table at the side of the room talking privately and a large table sits in the center. It's long enough to accommodate at least a dozen people but only half the chairs are being used.

The well-traveled ground is permanently imperfect, dips and divots detail the packed dirt. A partially worn path leads to the front of the table, right to the one person the Wanderers trust above all others.

Lord Raske sits at the head of the table and his commanding general, and son, Kaino, sits to his right. His second in command, and most surprisingly loyal subject, Declan sits to his left. No one here trusts the hybrid and yet their leader does. The three of them speak in a quiet and serious tone, a static buzz courses through the room from the sound of their hushed voices.

Though Declan is silently despised among the Wanderers, he has his lord's highest respect. Declan was a wanderer long before the government established a community to dump them all into and he helped Lord Raske raise this village into the powerful and self-reliant foundation that it is today.

What everyone is well aware of though, is that a decade of success isn't something to cheer about. Our community is young and has enemies all around. Including the ones who granted us our secret freedom.

Confidently, I step up to the opposing end of the table and force myself to pull my hands behind my back in a military stance. *A stance Ky took thousands of times.* I swallow the thought down and keep my eyes trained on Lord Raske and no one else. My spine straightens, my chin held high, my eyes respectful but unwavering.

Out of the corner of my eye, I can see the surrounding members of the table focus on me; Kaino, Declan and finally Lord Raske.

Lord Raske fills the end of the table, his heavy frame leaning into the old wood, testing the strength of the structure as he presses his large forearms onto the top. His black hair is trimmed close, flecks of gray are scattered throughout. His eyes, so like his sons, stare back at me, a glint of a predator present within the depthless dark irises.

"Fallon, I'm happy to see you enjoying our festivities this evening." A creasing smile fills the lord's round jovial face. "Do you need Kaino for anything? We'd be willing to spare him." He laughs a booming echo, his happiness shaking his wide body, and the majority of the mystics join him. Except for Kaino and Declan.

Lord Raske is pushing Kaino and I together, like two birds in a small, small cage. I blink harshly and struggle to form a slight smile on my tight lips. The false emotions my mother taught me to use to my advantage are fading and are hard to recall when needed.

With Lord Raske's stature and loud jarring voice, it comes as a surprise that he is a kind and reassuring leader but rejection hurts even with the gentlest of words.

"Thank you, Lord Raske, but I was hoping to speak with you, actually," I say as neutrally as possible, ignoring the offer of his son that he has thrown at my feet like rotten tomatoes from a heckler. Lord Raske raises his thick eyebrows encouragingly, although he and I both know what I'm about to say. "I would like to help in our militia, even if it's just the search and rescue teams to help find new people. People like me. I've been working with Luca for nearly a year now and my combat skills have improved drastically." My breathing threatens to increase like my pounding heartbeat but I take even breaths to calm myself.

Kaino shifts in his seat, the muscles of his wide shoulders tensing, and he looks away toward the blemished spindle leg of the table. Declan glances at Raske out of the corner of his silver eyes. Both commanders remain silent. Lord Raske's attention never leaves my face but his smile falters, slipping at the corners.

We've had this same conversation so often I'm starting to feel like I'm trapped in time here. Day in and day out I work in the clinic during the morning and I train with Luca in the evening. I'm allowed to help in stations of the community wherever I like throughout the rest of the day. I'm welcome to join community activities and sports, but I'm not to leave the grounds unattended until my training has met Lorde Raske's approval. I want and need to do something worthwhile.

I need to find him. Or whatever's left of him. My stomach turns with the dark thought as if I might throw up all the alcohol I've dumped into it this evening.

Until I find Asher's body and lay it to rest like my mother's, I won't be at peace. I hate that the word body is in my thoughts. So lifeless and hollow sounding. *He could be alive,* I remind myself as I swallow hard. My tongue is thick in my dry mouth, making speech feel impossible.

Luca went back for my mother's body the moment I told her what happened but Asher's wasn't there...

"I checked in on your training a few nights ago." Lord Raske pauses and my jaw is painfully tight while I try to wait for him to finish. "You have shown improvement." Another breezy smile flashes my way before he continues. "Unfortunately, you're just not where you need to be yet. I know you have it in you to join the militia."

My breathing is coming in heaps now and my jaw is screaming in pain at how tightly I have it closed.

"I just don't want to risk anyone's lives by sending you out too early. I wish you'd reach out to a few other *men,*" he emphasizes the word for my benefit. "To get more experience in other combat styles. You are at a disadvantage with your genetics, no fault of your own of course. I see the power, and possibly anger even, you hold within you." He studies me like a teacher looking at a studious student. "I want you out there, Fallon, I just don't want to risk you before you're ready."

Rapid blinking is all I can seem to manage. Part of me understands he's right, but an irrational part of me is furious that I'm being rejected. *Again.* I can't continue walking these overcrowded grounds. Continue being stared at and thought of as someone's future wife. The pressure to change their lives, my camp's lives, to change history, is so pressing I can't breathe.

I can't reach out to other males in the village because they don't want to train me. They want to wed me and get on with our lives. I'm stuck in time but so is everyone else, waiting on me. Waiting for me to make a choice. For me to make the easy choice and accept Kaino already.

My eyes dart to Kaino for just a second, seeking an ally. He sits assessing the drink in his hand, subtly turning the cup back and forth as the alcohol sways within. Not participating in the discussion. Not acknowledging me as a friend in the least.

The thoughts drench my mind in a wave of cluttered emotion but I realize I'm still standing before Lord Raske and I have yet to respond to his kind and thorough words.

"Thank you for your feedback, Lord Raske," I reply, still forcing myself to keep eye contact.

The conversation starts up again at the small table near the exit. I give a short nod and pivot in one swift motion to leave the stifling tent, my boots digging into the dirt as I forcefully turn.

"Meet me tomorrow morning at dawn, Fiercely."

Declan's voice is heard from behind me, my last name is said in a quiet breath and I pause to look at him. To really look at him for the first time since I arrived almost a year ago. His fingers tap soundlessly on the polished wooden table and he doesn't look up at me as he speaks. "There will be no more sleeping in for you. I'll drop our training in an instant if you prove to waste my time." His voice is strong and commanding. The opposite of the charming and flirty tone I'm used to hearing from him.

It's so different, I'm shocked at his proposal. I give him another short nod, closing my gaping mouth. His gaze holds mine for a few seconds, showing a lifetime of anger behind beautiful silver eyes.

THREE
THE ATTACK

I CLIMB down the rope from my bunk that hides high up in the trees. The tree bunks are for the Wanderers that want their own space, away from the endless celebrations and congested community of huts. The strange sleeping bunk is now the solitary place that I call my home.

The rough rope is still damp with morning dew and I struggle to make it safely to the ground as my boots slip, my muscles straining for support. My fingers ache from the amount of pressure I'm putting on them to hold tightly as I make my way to the forest floor.

The coloring of the sky is balancing in that struggling state between darkness and light. Water paint colors streak the heavens, slipping calm into my messy mind from the very sight of it. The moon is just starting to fade away to make room for the rising sun but it can still be seen if you look hard enough.

Through the soundless trees and past the now empty

grounds where last night's celebration was held, not a footprint is left behind to trace the event. But that is the way of the Wanderers. Even the tree pallets within the forest are hidden from view. Humans occasionally come through looking for food or a lost child but no one ever discovers the secret community that's shrouded in invisibility magic. But it's there. It exists. *We exist.*

The training circle welcomes my quiet steps, an area just within the trees where the brush has been cleared and manicured. Luca and I have practiced here every day for nearly a year. I wonder how different Declan will be. I wonder if I'll keep my temper long enough to learn something from the hybrid. I can keep my hatred for him separate from my training. At least for a month. Two weeks tops... Maybe we'll just see how today goes first.

I stretch my arms above my head, the weight of the Crimson Sword bumping familiarly against my thigh, as the sun starts to make its appearance on the horizon. I glance around the large clearing, the mounds of tangled brush that have been pushed to the sidelines of the makeshift training area, and listen for any approaching footsteps. The forest is a fortress of silence as if not even the wildlife is ready to climb out of bed. I roll my eyes at Declan's tardiness. How very like him to be late on our first day after mocking me about sleeping in.

A long and tired sigh drifts over my lips and I'm just turning to pace the length of the clearing when a weight falls from the trees above, landing jarringly on my shoulders and I'm pushed to the ground face first. My breath leaves my lungs in a whoosh. I struggle against strong arms as my wrists are jerked painfully back and held in one hand. My assailant leans his weight onto his other arm next to my head.

I'm still struggling against the person with no success when Declan's gray eyes meet mine. I grow still beneath him and attempt to blow a leaf and my tangled hair out of my face to look at him through a glare.

"Raske is right. You're not ready, love," he whispers to me through my wild hair, reveling in the successful attack he clearly planned.

Anger pushes through my veins with every labored breath I take. He just ruined my morning and I intend to repay him.

Without saying a word, I fling my head back hard and crack him in the nose. The noise is a sickening sound that lingers in my mind as pain soars through my skull but my anger doesn't allow the hurt to surface on my face.

With swift movements I leap to my feet, my dark boots breaking twigs under foot. I'm above him in a matter of seconds while he lies on his back, resting against one arm, holding his bloody nose in his other hand. My sword is drawn and rests at his neck, right where Asher slashed his own throat such a long, long time ago. My hand is steady as my scowl settles down on him.

"Clearly, Raske hasn't seen your best work yet." He wipes the blood from his already healing nose, leaning up fearlessly into the blade.

Perfect. His broken nose is flawlessly healed while the back of my head still throbs in pain. I'll probably have a headache for the rest of the day, while he had a broken nose for less than a minute. Blood smears across his smug face, tarnishing his unusual beauty. Overall it was worth it.

Lowering the blade, I sheath it at my side before extending my hand to help him stand. He's taller than I am and I force myself to look up at him with something mirroring respect. My stomach sinks with the familiarity of his features, like a glimpse of a memory in walking form, and I have to look away before the feeling consumes me and drags me under.

I wait for him to lead the training. I try not to *waste his time*. But we're just standing in silence as he works his jaw back and forth in thought. The silence is tingling through my nervous system and setting me on edge. I have to be at the clinic for work when it opens in less than two hours. When Luca and I train, I'm usually sweating and complaining by now. Waste *his* time. What a joke.

"Why did you volunteer to train me?" I ask to fill the active silence.

I want to ask what he intends to train. Why hasn't the training started yet? Maybe his little ambush approach was all he had mapped out for the day and he thought I would have already thrown in the towel. But here we stand. Me with a pressing headache and him with a perfectly healed, unbroken nose.

"I..." He pauses looking into the orange sky. The

colors reflect and make his eyes appear as burning flames. "I didn't want to," he says with a half-smile, his head shaking slightly.

His honesty catches me off guard and I can't help the way my brows dip in irritation and confusion.

"I didn't mean to offend you. It's just – Just that I've watched Kaino prance around you for a year. *A year*. That's an extraordinarily long time to waste with someone you have no intention of helping," he says quietly without looking at me. His words sink into my mind as I try to follow his meaning. "You've addressed your training with Lord Raske several times and every time Kaino just sits there, like a rock waiting to be thrown, waiting to be used in some way. Waiting for your rejection so we can all move on with our day."

I can't think of a thing to say in reply and Declan doesn't allow me to as he continues on.

"I'm not saying Kaino is a bad guy. He's not. But he shows interest in you because he wants to join with you to better our society," He stares me dead in the eyes now, "yet he doesn't even have the courage to help the person who intends to help him."

His words are spoken softly, bracingly. But they hit me hard. My heart hurts and my stomach sinks as I repeat his words in my mind. Kaino isn't in love with me, maybe we're not even friends. Declan is right. How many times has Raske told me I needed a male's training perspective and Kaino couldn't even look me in the face when his father dismisses my requests to help the militia?

"So I volunteered, not because I wanted to train you, but because I wanted to help you when no one else would. Because we're friends and I know what it's like to not have anyone's help. Not that I need it," he says with a wink.

He starts unbuckling his weapons belt from his slim waist and tosses it near the tree line. His sword clatters to the ground when the leather belt lands in the brush.

I nod at his words, trying to dissolve the hurt that floats in my chest. My face is neutral and my breathing is steady once again.

"All my kindness aside," he says with a smirk, "how about you take off that morbid sword and face me like a man?" I glare at him out of the corner of my eye but it doesn't fade his arrogant smile.

I unbuckle my belt that hangs loosely at my small waist. The worn leather weights my palm. I feel lighter and more vulnerable without the sword and all that it represents. Like a piece of my vital shelter has been stripped away from me in a rainstorm and I'm left defenseless to the world.

Declan's eyes light up with pure happiness as the crystal sword is no longer brushing my hip and his brilliant white teeth glisten as a broad smile spreads across his face. I gently place the weapon next to his sword and return to face him.

He pushes his shaggy blonde hair from his face, all seriousness returning to him. "How well can you fight?" he asks, measuring me up and down with a quick look.

Luca and I have covered hand to hand combat briefly but she's better with knives and other weapons, especially daggers. Our training is the reason I've started carrying a dagger, not that I'm the best with it. I think through the few times I have fought hand to hand with Luca and it didn't go well for me, but I refuse to tell Declan this.

"I'm experienced," I say, raising my chin. A vague reply, one my mother would be proud of.

Declan closes his eyes and slowly blinks at me. "Our training will only be successful and, quite honestly, will move a lot faster if you're just straightforward with me, Fallon," he says my name in a breath and the familiarity of it sends a chill tracing down my spine. I blink the memory back and give a short nod.

"I'm not very good," I tell him with my head held high, forcing my unsureness from my features.

He nods in understanding and his eyes dance across the dusty ground in thought.

"There's no shame in that," he tells me, facing me. "Let's start with basic self-defense. Raske wanted you trained by a male because males think differently. It's not sexist, it's a fact. Physically we're built different, we use our bulk to our advantage. The majority of combat soldiers are men. Even if you are a female it's important and beneficial to know how males – the enemy – think." He's naming off facts in a lecture like manner and I'm suddenly aware that the hybrid who shamelessly flirts with me is not the same scholarly like warrior that stands before me now.

"Today I'm going to have you attack me and I will slowly show you how to deflect the moves."

"What if I hurt you?" I ask without much thought.

A smile fills his features and he comes closer to me, leaving less than a foot of space between us. I stare up at him through dark lashes. The burning colors of the sky cast around him like an archangel. "I promise you, I won't break, love," he whispers against my hair.

Just when I thought my flirtatious friend had been replaced by a true Wandering Warrior, his breath fans over my face with a voice filled with smooth gravel.

"Similar to the defensive stance you hold with a sword, you will want to keep your feet braced apart, they should be a little farther out than your hips." I follow his instruction as he speaks and he watches me for error. This is similar to what Luca has said in our past training. "Your stance starts at your feet and your feet are the most significant factor in fighting." I glance up from my focus on my oh-so-important feet.

"You're kidding me, right?"

Another annoying smile tilts his lips and it occurs to me he might actually be enjoying bossing me around. He may actually like teaching someone his craft.

"Your feet hold your balance. Though your fists hold power, little good they will do if you're fumbling to the ground after every blow," he says, pushing my shoulder. He suppresses a laugh when I stumble out of my weak stance. My eyes narrow at him but he continues describing the best defensive stance, ignoring my glare entirely.

We spend about an hour working through and explaining fighting stances. I no longer question what he says and it's clear to me he has an extensive background in hand to hand combat.

He finishes walking me through how to properly hold my arms while fighting and how to dodge hits without moving my feet and we are now starting in on the actual physical training.

Declan puts one hand against my forehead, angling my head back, holding me to his chest like a hostage, and his other is empty but held at my throat in a mock knife-like manner. His strong body lines up behind my own. He moves slowly, making sure I'm aware of every movement.

Descriptions of every possible weak angle my attacker leaves open while in this position are spoken in a lecturing voice; the obvious exposed torso that provides infinite kill spot possibilities, his head that's close to my own but a bit too risky of a target considering the mock knife at my throat.

I take note of where his hands are placed, how his body is open behind me, how easy I could take the attacker down.

Then I'm suddenly aware of how his body is pressed against mine.

Sliding his hand from my neck down my arm, he jerks me against him as he walks us backward. "Your attacker may seem in control with how his build dominates over your own but always be aware of what he leaves open. The vulnerable space he's allowing by holding his arms high to manipulate your body."

My breathing hitches, and for just a moment my heart skips a beat, a shiver slipping over my skin from his touch. Abruptly, I realize how alone I've kept myself. It's like I've forgotten what it feels like to be held by anyone. Even in the threatening way Declan is intending for this position to be, I can't help but think how strong his chest and arms feel. How his arms are holding me against him, like a claim almost.

His breath feathers over my damp neck as he speaks. "Fallon, are you listening to me?" he asks, dropping his arms restlessly to his sides and leaning around me to look in my eyes, taking his warmth with him.

Emotions storm through me so fast I can't keep up. A flush fills my face from how ridiculous my feelings just became. I pull farther away from him before he can see the strange thoughts that are probably written all over my red face. I take a couple deep breaths before walking away altogether and start buckling my sword back to my waist.

"Sorry," I refuse to look at him, to raise my heat-filled face to him. "I forgot it's my day to open the clinic. I can't be late."

Out of the corner of my eye, I see him raise his palms at my odd behavior but I still can't look at him.

"Thanks for working with me. I'll see you tomorrow."

A nervous smile twitches against my lips as I start to walk quickly toward the camp. "Same time?" I ask over my shoulder. I nod at him even though he's still looking at me in confusion and I don't give him enough time to answer my question before I'm hurrying away into the trees.

The Wanderer's clinic is the only building in the community that isn't hidden up high in the trees or deep in the forest. I spend every day here helping and working under Doctor Thierry, a witch in her mid-forties. She seems to appreciate herbal remedies more than magic, a fact that sets me at ease, finally something familiar that I excel at.

She reminds me of my mother for some reason. They have no resemblance really, just two women who are both doctors. I suppose I'm forcing my mother's absence into physical form. But I can't help it.

Doctor Thierry's kind and everyone that walks into the unmarked building loves her. Me on the other hand, they seem wary of. A new face isn't always welcome when people have been going to the same trusted doctor for all of their lives. But I'm a fast learner and Doctor Thierry always tells everyone how grateful she is to have such an experienced apprentice.

I'm just finishing wrapping an older fae's leg that had been sliced open on the side of a cliff when Declan walks slowly into the clinic. He's hesitantly looking around the one room building when his mystical eyes meet mine. I give my patient a small smile when he says thank you, taking the bag of medicine and additional gauze Dr. Thierry gave him. The patient gives Declan a scowl on his way out, a watchful glare thrown toward the hybrid.

In the quietest of growls the fae speaks as if spitting down on the hybrid as he passes. "*Pike.*"

I flinch, jarred from the impact of the simple but angry statement. Declan appears to overlook the hate slur, his hands in his pockets, eyes cast down in apparent thought. A heavy feeling presses into my chest as I swallow hard, blinking up at him.

The doctor is writing in her large charting book she carries with her and her pencil scratching softly against the paper is the only noise that can be heard in the quietness.

Declan looks out of place in the small white tiled room. His natural light complexion and black shirt and cargo jeans cast severely against the white walls. A dryness consumes my throat and I swallow harshly to clear it. I try to appear busy, cleaning up the old bandages and wiping down my table.

Dr. Thierry's head slowly tilts up, seeming to feel the anxious silence all around us. A look passes from me to Declan, waiting to hear what he needs.

"Could I, um- Could I speak with you for a minute?" he asks, finally looking at me. He shifts his stance, finding his confidence again.

A nervousness fills my body, tensing my shoulders and limbs and settling into my sweating, unoccupied hands. I shouldn't have overreacted about our training this morning. He was trying to help me and my mind went to a place it hasn't wandered to in so long, I had forgotten it even existed at all.

I glance to Dr. Thierry and start to ask if I can take a five-minute break but a look crosses the women's thin, smooth features. A strange, happy, knowing look. She looks Declan's lean body up and down before standing abruptly from her desk, the legs of her chair scraping against the tile. "Fallon, I'm going to run out to our storage and see if I can't find a few old files I've been meaning to update. I'll put the board back over the door while I'm gone so no one comes in. I shouldn't be more than fifteen minutes." She says as she flitters through the room with a cheerful smile.

I'm left gawking at her from my seat. She gives Declan a pleasant smile when she passes, pushing her wire rim glasses up her pert nose and walks right out the door. The thud, as the board that covers the abandoned looking building falls into place behind her, is the final note in her bizarre performance.

"That was strange," Declan says, his brow creased as he looks over his shoulder at the door.

A quietness settles over us again. I'm basically locked in a room with the last person I wanted to see again today and I have no idea what to say to him. He tilts his head and takes a look around the tiny space before his eyes settle back on me. At least I'm not the only one who doesn't know what to say.

"I've never actually been in here," he says nodding to himself. "It's... cleaner than I expected." His gaze appraises the shining floor and the small organized desk I sit at.

"It kind of has to be," I say, trying to fill the void of silence "Risk of infection and all."

He nods in agreement, with a little too much enthusiasm. I can't think of a thing to say but I also can't stop looking at him. The sharp angles of his face. His hair that constantly threatens to spill into his light eyes. The way his jeans hang loosely on his lean waist. I glance away at the last thought.

Why am I being so weird around him? Get ahold of yourself, Fallon.

He licks his lips and walks close to my table. The pen I'm holding falls to the floor with a small clicking sound. I don't pick it up but the noise of the plastic hitting tile clings in the silent air.

"I – I wanted to talk about this morning." He pauses, waiting for any recognition in my face but all I provide is a blank stare. Willing myself not to speak. "I'm sorry. If I made you uncomfortable, or if I hurt you." Again, he waits for me to respond and once again I offer nothing. "If I brought up old memories of how Luca found you. Of the night you got that scar. Of how we met..."

Concerned eyes search my face for confirmation, catching every detail of emotion I reveal. I open my mouth but say nothing. Instead, I cross my arms and secretly trace my fingers over the jagged line that etches over my ribs.

Memories of all the times Asher held me to him, safety enveloped around me as his strong arms pulled me against his chest. The night I got this scar, the night Luca found me, the night it all fell apart, Asher held me the way Declan did this morning. Like he'd never let me go. Like I'd never have to fear a world without him in it.

My throat bobs at the thoughts that involuntarily flood my mind. I force another dry swallow and keep my eyes on the floor instead of facing him.

"You didn't scare me, Declan. I've been in combat before, combat I wasn't prepared for, but I'm not that dying girl you saved a year ago." He tilts his head to try to meet my eyes but I shift in my seat until I'm angled away from him. "I just didn't expect to actually appreciate what you had to teach," I say a bit honestly. I have to give him an answer and this is as honest as I'm willing to be. "I'm sorry I misjudged you. You're a great teacher and I hope you'll continue teaching me."

A steady breath slips through my lungs, calming and reassuring, and I force myself to smile up at him. A look of false happiness etched into my straining features. His head tilts slightly and a beat passes between us before he finally nods. My stomach jars within at his easy acceptance. My pain magnifies internally while I keep my lips turned up in a sad smile—a look I've seen the hybrid give others countless times.

FOUR
A PROPOSAL

Declan keeps his word and continues to teach me hand to hand combat over the next couple of days. Muscles I didn't know existed ache throughout my body. My legs wobble beneath my steps. My arms shake when they lift from my sides. My sides that protest with every movement. A good sign that Declan's doing his job. I still continue to avoid the nightly celebrations the best I can. Luckily, Kaino hasn't ventured out to drag me to one, either.

It's a rather nice routine I've settled into, actually. Every morning just before dawn I train with Declan, keeping my emotions placid and my attention on my own body. In the afternoon I work at the clinic, filling my time even though it is incredibly slow. I guess that's expected when the majority of the population heals themselves. And in the evenings I eat dinner with Luca. It's boring but simple.

I'm just smirking to myself as I send a strike to Declan's jaw, which he dodges, as easily and annoyingly as he does every day, but I catch him off guard and he stumbles to the dirt, flat on his back. Achievement washes over me. Maybe I didn't land the punch but my surprise attack paid off. It's so rare that I ever get the upper hand on the hybrid that the adrenaline from my minor success overtakes my thoughts. Happiness and pride burn through my veins and I can't help but close my eyes and smile into the warm sunlight as sweat trails down my neck.

Within moments, my feet are kicked out from under me and I land hard on my side right next to him, dirt flying up all around me. Sharp pain floods my limbs and jars my teeth.

His angled features curve up in a delighted smile toward the morning sky that I was just worshiping a moment earlier. "Always celebrating too soon, love."

The pain shooting through my arm and my ribs intensify and I suppress a groan. It's obvious I'm Dr. Thierry's most recurring patient. She'll be horrified when I ask her to take a look at my arm that might possibly be fractured. My injuries never seem to cross Declan's mind. He's so used to his natural healing abilities and those of the Wandering Warrior's, he clearly hasn't got a clue how fatally human I am.

"I have a proposal for you," Declan tells me, glancing at me out of the corner of his eye, his chest rising and falling minimally.

All thoughts of my arm and ribs push from my mind immediately. A proposal? His words are so serious I suddenly want to run away again. I can count the number of times Declan has been serious with me and that number doesn't even fill one hand.

"I'm listening."

An intake of breath, loud and heavy, passes his lips like he's gathering the courage to say something. I try to keep a bored expression in my features but my mind is reeling with each second that ticks by.

"I was hoping you'd stop working at the clinic after our training each day." He pauses to meet my eyes before continuing. My brows rise at his choice of topic. "If you were to be my understudy, Raske would be more apt to take you more seriously and you would, in turn, get what you wanted. On a smaller scale, of course, there are still some restrictions." He's looking back at the few scattered clouds filling the sky again and I can see him visibly swallow, his Adam's apple struggling to accommodate such a calm task.

Lying on my side, my mouth opens but then closes just as fast, unsure how to respond. He just offered me what I've been pleading for with Raske for months. An understudy. A loophole is what it really is. Why is he offering this to me? Declan could have any member of our community be his understudy and most of them wield unnatural strength that would fare a thousand times better than myself.

"W-Why?" I sputter.

He laughs, a flash of white on display within his perfect smile.

"I mean, of course, I appreciate the offer, but why would you want me? I'd be more work than I'm worth." Bitter honesty stings my voice.

He rolls onto his side to face me. Crystal-like eyes search my face, a frown shadowing his features. His arm rests under his head and his other hand taps restlessly against his leg.

"Because we're friends, Fallon." He takes a breath, his prowling eyes travel the length of the thick forest in thought before returning to me. "I know I flirt with you and tease you because you're one of the few people that tolerate speaking to me, but I mean it when I say we're friends. At least you are to me. You don't look at me the way every single person that I pass looks at me. Only Raske has ever shown me kindness, a kindness his son didn't inherit. I've roamed city to city and I've been dumped out of every one of them except here. This screwed up society accepts and rejects me all at the same time." He closes his eyes for a moment. Flinching at his own words, while the pain that he's kept inside sinks into me.

"But you don't look at me like they do. Your eyes don't hold anger or disgust at what I am. I don't know where you came from, because I've been all over and I've never met someone that makes me feel—" A hesitancy fills him, seemingly thinking through his feelings. "You make me feel like I'm actually alive."

Like he's alive. Something so simple. Like I can see him as a person, not a hybrid, a *pike.* The derogatory term for his kind is heavy in my mind. There are mystics of all kinds, none are accepted by humans but his race is hunted. The pain he transfers into me radiates and spreads through me as I recall all the times I've rolled my eyes or said a snide remark to him. I'm not exactly kind to him. He's just as lost as I am.

Maybe we all are.

Everyone in this community is here because society couldn't allow them to be who they are. Because they were tired of changing or hiding who they really were to better bend to the form of those around them. But they still want this hybrid to bend in hopes that he will break. So they can sweep up the pieces and dump them in a corner of their mind that they will revisit with guilty souls but clear minds.

But he won't.

Swallowing hard, I try to make sense of his confession. "You confuse the hell out of me, Declan," My words pull a small smile over his lips, "but anyone should be honored to be your understudy. I accept and appreciate your offer," I say as formally as he originally did.

His smile widens, genuine happiness settles into his smooth features. The sky becomes his focus as he seems absorbed in his thoughts, his smile slips away by the second.

"Really, thank you," I whisper.

The transition from clinic assistant to militia understudy happens quickly and with a strange ease. To be honest, I'm forcing it to happen with ease. I follow Declan like a quiet and observant shadow, taking mental notes of details he feeds me; who is in charge of what, what assignments we take care of daily, when search and rescues are scheduled – highlighted mental note for that one – and in general, it isn't that hard. Declan treats me as an equal. There's no flirty context in his voice, no lingering glances, no teasing at all. Just one soldier to another.

Kaino, on the other hand, stares at me daily, seemingly confused and frustrated by this subtle change in his routine.

"You want to take her on tomorrow's search? Someone who hasn't even had a month's worth of real training?" Kaino growls, his brows pulled low, shadowing his dark eyes.

I stand in silence at Declan's side, once again the newcomer in their society. The busy warriors around me glance our way but say nothing as they pack their bags for tomorrow's trip—well, almost all of them... Luca stops packing and now stands tall with her hands firmly on the curve of her hips, glaring at her brother.

"That is exactly what I want to do, because Private Fiercely isn't a pedestrian, she's one of our own. She's had the training and the knowledge to begin shadowing search expeditions, Sir," Declan says, holding Kaino's glaring gaze.

I raise my chin, folding my hands neatly behind my back, trying to find the confidence and respect Ky always seemed to have.

A small, distant part of me wants to brush away this hostility and simply say I will wait until Kaino believes I'm ready, but the painful need to find Asher is stronger. I'm not the person I was a year ago and I will not cower from the things I deserve. I deserve to be included in my own life.

The two of them stare in silence for a few seconds, careful not to tip the balance of peace and power that this society teeters on. Declan raises his hand, his palm clasping Kaino's shoulder, a pleading look touching the hybrid's eyes. His hand rests against Kaino's skin for mere seconds before the commander's look turns from annoyed to aggressive, as he jerks away from Declan's simple touch. Kaino's eyes glimmer in the sunlight, turning a lighter shade of amber, almost gold before he blinks it away, pushing the animal back into the cage it's always kept in. A cage forced so tightly closed the bars are ready to break...

"If something happens to her," Kaino voice is low and promising as he sizes Declan up from head to toe, "I'll execute you myself, on my father's orders." He clenches his jaw shut and storms away, into the forest, the wolf returning to its den.

Declan releases a long breath and turns to me with a

wide smile, the boy-like grin that I haven't seen in days on display.

"He really needs to release all that pent up hostility," he says, nudging me with his elbow. "Pack your bag, love, don't want to miss this possibly once in a lifetime opportunity."

I nod, excitement pooling in my chest, finally leaving this haven and doing something instead of the eternal waiting I've grown so used to.

Once in a lifetime opportunity.

He's right. If anything, and I do mean anything, goes wrong tomorrow, I won't be given a second chance. So, I'll have to make the day trip count. Leave no rock unturned... Considering I'll be hunting a hybrid who lived the majority of his life under a refrigerator, our trip will definitely be harder than it seems.

FIVE
THE RED HILLS

THE FOLLOWING MORNING, just before the sun was touching the horizon, Declan led a small group along the rocky shore of the Emerald Ocean, through the thick, familiar forest and to a place called the Red Hills.

Declan, Luca, a wolf descendant named Shane, and I stand on the outskirts of the forest. Jagged red-gray mountains etch the sky in front of us, blocking out the morning sun. A strange fog of crimson casts along the dips and crevices of the area, seemingly reaching out to us.

My stomach drops as my mind processes where we are heading—standing literally at rock bottom— the only place to go is up, into the cursed Red Hills.

The exhausted part of me wishes I would have listened to Kaino and stayed at camp, while the determined part of me is ready to keep moving.

Luca adjusts her pack, which matches my own, heavy

but filled only with necessities. Shane takes a swig of water from his silver canteen, assessing the mountains, appearing to draw a route in his mind's eye.

"Luca, you and Shane take the direct route, Fallon and I will search the northern valleys and meet you on the other side, past Pike's Peak. We need to be across by midday to make our return by nightfall. We don't want to be in this area after sundown."

Pike's Peak.

The term strikes hard against my sternum, nearly knocking the air out of me. My eyes are wide, my mind reeling, barely hearing the rest of his instructions.

The clear sky appears endless as I watch Luca and Shane leave, crossing the dry plains toward the mountains. I stand unmoving, my eyes fixed on the sharp peaks touching the sky, shadowing the land around them.

What's hiding in the shadows of Pike's Peak? The few remaining vampires of this world? If the whispers of my camp were true then, yes, we're trailing the cursed cliffs of the hidden community of vampires...

"You coming?" Declan asks, looking back at me a few feet away.

I nod, pushing my thoughts from my mind, taking long steps to catch up to him, I turn my head, still watching Luca's figure grow smaller and smaller against the mountains. My boot catches on something, roughly pulling me to the ground. My hands brace my hard landing, my fingers pushing into the dirt, scraping roughly against the dry earth.

Declan stops in his tracks, smirking but offers me his hand. As he pulls me up I glance down at the dead tree branch that's littering the dirt, catching dry leaves and twigs and what appears to be paper.

Bending down, I pick up the foreign piece of paper, so out of place in nature. My fingers work meticulously to straighten the edges of the crinkly and torn document. Once its edges are smooth my breath leaves my lungs, leaving me gasping and confused.

My face stares back at me.

Against the dirty white paper are my own green eyes looking up at me, my dark hair pulled high and neatly atop my head, a broad smile stretched across my tan face.

It's my school ID photo, laying out here in the desert, ready to blow into the mountains and never be seen again.

Along the bottom of the page in stark bold letters are the words:

MISSING:
FALLON FIERCELY
LAST SEEN HEADED WEST
APPROACH WITH CAUTION
ANY INFORMATION SHOULD BE REPORTED
DIRECTLY TO YOUR
CONGRESSMAN, AYDEN THOMAS

Ayden.

His name stands out like the guiding moonlight in the clear night sky. *Is he searching for me?*

Of course he is.

How does he even know I never returned?

"*Caution*? What the hell does that mean?" Declan's pale blonde hair brushes against my temple as he scans over the paper.

"I don't know."

I do know.

It means Asher.

My mind rewords the true meaning in an instant: *Caution, the pike that she was last seen with isn't very well liked and is seen as a bloodthirsty killer. Could have just been blunt, Ayden.*

"Have you ever seen this before?" I ask, leaning away a little to look at him.

He pauses, searching my eyes.

"Yes."

"Where? How many?"

Declan exhales a long breath, raising his brows as he thinks. His slowness to respond makes the anticipation grow to a hulking mass in my chest.

"I don't know, a hundred, maybe two hundred copies scattered through the woods, throughout neighboring villages, the desert planes stretching between here and the Capitol."

"Two. Hundred. Copies." I take a deep breath, ready to blow out every word I know to try to express my anger.

"You passed two hundred copies of my grubby face thrown throughout the world like confetti and you didn't think to notify me? Maybe the missing person herself might want to know about this little bit of information."

"I-"

"You, what?" I yell, balancing on the toes of my black boots to get in his face. It doesn't work, he still towers over me.

"I was instructed not to," he says in an apprehensive voice, looking away from me, his eyes narrowing toward the mountain line.

I stumble on my feet, knocked back down to my small stature. Why would he be instructed not to tell me? Did Kaino tell him not to tell me? Why would he do that?

"Why?" The word is a whisper, the only one I can manage to speak.

"Raske wanted to wait. To present you like a prize during the Treaty Celebration."

"Why?"

His feet shift, his rifle falls pointing toward the dirt, no longer invested in the threats that may surround us.

"Because he wants to use you." My eyes flash to his face, but he doesn't look at me. "Everyone is looking for the girl that was stolen by the pike, Fallon. The pike that murdered her family and left nothing but a trail of dust in their wake. Raske wants to present you as an engaged human, uniting the races. A shiny prize that illuminates the oppression that the human society is kept from. Your village, that congressman Ayden, can't accept and announce your return unless they accept your biracial union, as well. This congressman has spread the word, caused a lot of attention for you and Raske wants to capitalize on it."

"My union?" I ask, my eyes raging as I stare up at him in shock and anger. He nods hesitantly at my simple question. "My union that doesn't even exist. Raske is using this nonexistent union to free his people. To crawl out of hiding in the hopes that people like me enough to accept a biracial union that isn't even real."

All this time, all this time they've taken me in and saved me and cared for me and built me up, just to structure me how they like—to use me.

"When you say it like that, it sounds kind of ridiculous," he smirks at me, defaulting to sarcasm even when he knows it won't help. He grows serious as he takes in my fallen features. "Everyone has an angle, love, you just have to make sure not to get hurt on their sharp edges."

The fog fills my sight everywhere I turn, tinged with red and filling my lungs like a vapor, clouding my mind. I follow Declan more closely the farther into the mountain's valley we climb.

The strange fog lingers around us, dancing with our feet as we wade through it, desperate for the other side.

"It's Crimson Mist. Back in the fifties, when the humans joined the fae and the warlocks in the war defeating the creatures of the night, the warlocks and witches cursed this land where so many of our people lost their lives. They fought and they died, but won." Declan glances around, sifting his fingers through the wafting red fog. "The human population was severely decreased, but lucky for you, your kind reproduces at an alarming rate, like an infestation really." I glare at him but he only smirks at me and continues on. "So the warlocks and witches cursed the Red Hills—Pike's Peak—deeming that the air will only be clean once all the creatures of the night have been cleansed of this earth."

I watch the mist swirl around us, Declan's gray eyes and pale features standing out amongst the thick red atmosphere.

"So they still live?" I ask.

"Of course they do. If you can call being trapped within the very thing that's killing you living. The Infinity witches cursed them here decades ago."

I arch an eyebrow at him, confused by his words, but he carries on with the tale.

"It's said that a few, and by few I mean, three withering, worthless, dying creatures are buried within the Red Hills, the crystal-like material that your sword is made from, is forged directly from the mountain that they're imprisoned in. Mystics can't even touch the mountain, it'll scar their skin just like the sword. The vampire's abilities are dying out within the darkness." He turns and continues walking, pulling himself up the red granite and farther into the valley.

I think through his words, a riddle seemingly present within their meaning.

"You've met them."

He stops, kneeling with one boot against the angled incline. His back is rigid, his muscular arms frozen in midair, holding on the rocky edge, ready to pull himself up but he doesn't.

He jumps down, scattering little rocks to the ground as he lands, staring at me.

"I need you to forget everything that just came out of my mouth," he says slowly, staring intensely at me as if his life depends on it.

And it does.

If anyone found out that Declan, *the pike*, had any kind of connection to the vampires, he'd be executed for treason.

"What are their abilities?" I ask, holding his gaze.

"I said forget it," he repeats.

I raise my chin and square my shoulders. I need this information. More than I've ever needed anything in my entire life and he's going to help me.

"You said you were my friend. I treated you like a friend while you let everyone around me plot and use me like I'm some kind of animal for their harvest. If these-" I pause, realizing how dangerous the idea is that is soaring to life in my mind. "If these vampires can help me find him," I don't say his name, I can't and I just have to hope Declan understands. "You have to tell me, Dec. Please." I nearly sob, my shaky breath parting the red mist.

He pauses, considering my words, absorbing the desperation in my eyes.

This is his moment and he knows it. He's helped me more than anyone ever has, he's saved my life, but he's also lied to me, concealed things from me, something a friend would never do. Deep in the back of my mind I know I'm pressing him too hard. Declan isn't familiar with people tolerating him, the idea of friendship is still foreign to him and I'm using that to my advantage but I can't walk away from this request.

"Fine. But follow my instructions, these things aren't something to play with. Mortals are exceptions to the magic here. The mortals started the rebellion and only a mortal can safely grace this land. I can't touch the cursed rock, I won't be able to help you if you don't listen to me."

Happiness explodes in my chest, a smile stretches across my face, tears almost spilling over my cheeks. My gratitude seems to make him uncomfortable and he looks away from me, his silver eyes searching the red mist around us. But before he turns to walk away—to lead the way to what could very well be our deaths—I fling my arms around him at the last minute. His strong shoulders tense under my touch and he doesn't immediately reciprocate the gesture. But I can feel it, I can feel the moment his guard lowers. He wraps one arm carefully around me, his hand is feather light against my back. He leans his head against mine, seemingly letting go of some of the pain I know he carries with him.

A slow breath feathers against my hair before he drops his hand from me and turns away. Shielding myself and everyone else from any sign of real feelings the hybrid might possess.

SIX
ATTICUS

THE RED MIST isn't as dense the farther into the valley we walk. I can now see the blue sky above, the sun burning through the curse to heat our backs as we heave ourselves through the steep inclines. We've trekked through the rocky trail for hours now. There's no way we're meeting Luca and Shane on time now. Will Declan tell them what held us up or will he lie for me? For us, really...

Declan stops abruptly and leans against a rock wall, tilting his head up as if praying to a God that may not even acknowledge his kind.

"Get the sword out, and don't hesitate for an instant. Don't show your fear, swallow it down, stomp it out, don't let it come to life here. Because they'll know, they'll feed off of it like vultures. This is the only interaction with a human they might get for the rest of their lives. They'll say whatever they can think of to claw into your mind or tear your defenses down long enough to kill you, which wouldn't be long at all." He speaks quickly and I try to catch each instruction he gives me. "One last thing," my eyes are wide as if I can visually capture every word, "they'll ask for your hand, and you'll give it to them if you truly want what they can offer."

"My hand?" My fingers twitch at my sides, nerves settling in at my fingertips.

With a nod, he looks away and I swallow, trying to ease the panic that just flooded my chest. I pull out the Crimson Sword in one swift motion. The feel of it heavy in my hand diminishes my fears. I follow behind Declan, matching his casual gait the best I can.

Our steps are cautious but announcing as rock shifts beneath our every move. The air grows thicker with each step we take within the mountains. The mist and something else is clouding my lungs. Something pungent and repulsing fills the air and makes me choke back my shallow breaths.

"Ah, the golden boy returns to us," a taunting and raspy voice says.

Declan stops just in front of a large pile of boulders blocking an opening within a towering mountain, bits of gray and white peak through the dusty blood red film that's overlaying the rock.

"Atticus, how are the peaks treating you these days?" Declan asks, his gun lowering at his side as if he feels at home here.

"Better today," the voice—Atticus says, coming from a

small gap between the red rock. "It's not every day someone brings us something so pretty to look at." I remain impassive, just watching the dark shadows between the rocks, waiting for a glimpse of the vampire locked within. "What do you want, girl?"

With cautious steps, I move closer, almost close enough to reach out and touch the shadows. My heart pounds in my chest but I try to keep my shallow breaths steady.

"I'm looking for someone and I've come to you for guidance," I say as respectfully as possible.

"Hmmmm." Fear begins to implode in my chest at the hesitant hum of his ancient voice. Not fear of Atticus, but fear that he might not help me at all. "Give me your hand, girl."

I hold the sword tightly in my fist, the beams of sun reflecting wildly off of the shining blade, as I extend my hand toward the shadowy opening. Heart-racing fear gives me the energy to flee but my feet remain immobile. I don't look to Declan for guidance as I slip my left hand through the tight space.

A cold skeletal like hand drifts over my skin and I suppress a shudder, my chest heaves up and down, fully taking in the decaying stench that clings to the air. Countless fingers trail over my hand, stroking my palm but only one voice dares to speak, or maybe the other two aren't strong enough... I blink rapidly, trying my best not to pull away from their jagged nails that are raking softly over my skin.

"The hybrid you seek has not sought us out, but I can see him." Another careful and jagged nail rakes across my knuckles. "He's close, within walking distance." Cold leathery flesh touches the back of my hand and the vampire inhales my scent, his nose and dry lips scrape over my skin, making my heart want to leap out of my chest. "I can almost smell him on you, and if you breathed deep enough you could probably smell him within these mountains, as well."

Louder my heart pounds in my ears, fear starting to consume my mind, and I fight back the urge to inhale the deathlike air around me.

"I wonder if you'd still be as pretty if I skinned you alive and wore your corpse out of here like a raincoat in the sweltering sunlight."

"That's enough," Declan growls, jerking my arm back so hard his nails sink into me. "Thank you for your valuable time, gentlemen."

Declan walks away without another word, the opposite way we came. But I stand watching, holding my hand to my chest, my flesh feeling alive where they've clawed at my skin. I stare wide-eyed into the dark hole. The sun shines down on me, and through the mist that hangs in the air, through the shadows of the darkness, the sun's beautiful rays illuminate a single, haunting red eye staring right at me.

It's late when Declan and I return. The night has grown heavy, the moon held high in the sky, surrounded by endless twinkling stars, but the community is alive with music and laughter. My steps don't slow as I storm into the war tent. Raske gives me a warm smile that seems to melt his dark chocolate gaze. Kaino glances to me, ignoring my rage filled eyes as he finishes his discussion with his father.

I've had hours to dwell on what Declan confessed to me and the longer we walked the more I wanted to rip this place apart, the place I've called my home for the past year. The leader I've looked to for guidance and honesty has lied to me every day for a year.

"You want to use me to find peace between the mortals and the mystics?"

The dozen or so warriors within the room stop to appreciate my outburst. Some of them just leave, choosing to walk away while they have the chance. Declan clears his throat behind me but my aggression won't allow me to acknowledge him. My heart beats almost painfully as I wait for Raske to say something.

Raske glances around the room at the few stragglers, nodding at them in silence. They trail from the room one by one until it's just the four of us alone in the stifling tent.

"I'm not using you, Fallon. None of us are using anyone. If you were to accept one of my men, accept my own son even, the gesture of a human loving a mystic would be enough to change the world. Do you understand that? With your help, we could change the world. All it takes is one person to lead as an example." His gentle but deep voice fills the room. "You aren't like other mortals, Fallon. You see us as your equal. With the attention your friends and camp have put on your disappearance, others would take notice of your choices. It would be slow, but change can happen."

My lungs heave as I take in angry gulps of air. Slowly, I try to calm my shaking fists and twitching jaw as I stare at him.

He's right. I know he is. A mortal sharing a lifetime of happiness with a mystic could be the first steps to ending the segregation... It's just faking a lifetime of happiness that's the problem.

If I were to accept any one of his men. I consider asking him if a hybrid like Declan would be acceptable in his plan—the race that not even the mystics accept fully—but I know the answer. Kaino is the number one choice. He's the right choice. Yet, he can't even look at me during this discussion. He has nothing to say in my defense.

More anger boils over the almost calm surface that I tried so hard to find. I clench my fists tightly closed, turn on my heels and exit the tent. The fury I'm holding on to is expelled from my body in a breath of surprise as I collide with someone else, my head banging harshly against their chest.

I run my fingers over my sore forehead as a familiar dog whines at my feet. He's odd looking with matted fur and one little ear ends in jagged, scarred flesh. My heart drops and then leaps in my chest as I bend down to pick up the excited animal that was once my best friend. Ripper wiggles in my arms, I stand, hugging the restless dog and sorrow fills me as my fingers rub the damaged ear that's almost entirely missing. Rapid and endless laps of his tongue meet my knuckles and arms and anything in his reach. My head dips toward his and I'm met with the most pungent smell that's clinging to his fur.

What has he been rolling in over the last year? How did he get here?

My eyes finally drift to the person I bumped into and my heartbeat stammers, a gasp tearing from my lips as I meet his astonished gaze. I'm face to face with the one person I've thought about day and night for the past year.

Asher.

SEVEN
A FORMAL INTRODUCTION

FROM ACROSS THE flames of the fire, Nerissa laughs loudly over the rhythmic drums, sending a jolt of annoyance through me from the sight of her charming smile. Her long waves of emerald hair brush against Asher's shoulder. My heart violently pounds against my chest with every beat of the drum, with every smile she gives him. Anger thrums closer to the surface with every charming smile he gives her in return.

The only real happiness I've felt since seeing Asher is the wide-eyed look the children gave me when I introduced the little Wanderers to Ripper. Their little hands appreciated his dirty fur and excited kisses as if he was the most amazing, filthy animal that had ever crawled out of the forest.

And he is.

The children keep the happy dog busy, feeding him every scrap of food they can find, giving him a long bath and playing with him for hours. Now he naps in the arms of a pleased fae child, the curve of her smile is highlighted in the flames as she stares down at the tiny sleeping animal.

I can't believe the dog trusted Asher for the last year. That he finally stopped growling at him long enough to follow the hybrid to safety.

The cute image holds my attention for a single minute before Nerissa's laughter breaks into my thoughts again, my eyes darting toward them once more.

"I found the two of them walking the Red Hills. It's him, isn't it?" Luca asks in a quiet voice, pausing only a moment before realizing I won't answer. "Can you believe that fae slut?" she asks, her eyes following my trance and watching Nerissa as her hand touches Asher's bicep for the third time, laughing again at whatever clever thing he's saying.

I take a drink from my cup, the liquid burns down my throat and settles in at home with the fire that's flooding my chest. I try to pull my eyes away from the sight of him, but I can't.

We stared at each other for minutes, his silver eyes tracing every inch of my body until my pounding heart was struck with fear. *What if Raske doesn't accept another hybrid?* Declan already puts the Wanderers on edge and my history with Asher could threaten the lord's plans.

So, I let Raske and the rest of our community think that Asher and Gabriel are strangers to me, out of panic of getting them pushed out of the Wandering community. I moved past him without a second glance, my chest shaking with unshed tears the whole time.

"Really, walk on water and behold the magic of the sea, and suddenly you're the most enthralling person they've ever met?" Luca's icy tone causes me to finally look away from Asher. I steal a glance at my friend and find that she, too, is seething at the shameless flirting that's happening just in front of us. I watch Luca a little longer. Her lip curls in disgust as Nerissa runs her thin fingers through Gabriel's red hair and it's then that I realize he's different. One hand holds his drink, his shoulders stiff from the attention of the water fae, while his other hand... is missing. Just a little above his wrist the limb ends in nothing but smooth skin.

My stomach sinks low but I try to focus on Luca for a moment.

"You like him?" I say slowly, my eyes lighting up for the first time since I saw Asher earlier tonight.

She coughs into her cup as she chokes on her alcohol, her face scrunching into a look of pain. Declan stops at my side, smirking at Luca who attempts to find a normal breath.

"No, not at all. I just think it's embarrassing how the water fae is throwing her tang at anyone now. Do you know what she looked like when she first came here?" A disgusted and dramatic shiver runs over my friend's body.

I laugh a little too loudly at the remark, surprising even myself. Warm and slightly petty revenge settles in my chest at her words. Declan laughs with us and finds the target of our anger within the crowd.

"And here I thought fish analogies were below you two," Declan says, smirking at me from over his cup, his silver gaze once again painful for me to look at. Luca rolls her eyes at his remark.

"You know what they look like in the water. Those hybrids are in for a surprise if she ever lures them back to the sea," Luca says with a huff.

Across the fire, Asher looks at me for the first time since I brushed him off. The pain that soars through me plummets into the pit of my stomach like a comet obliterating the earth, and the smile on my lips falters.

He looks from Declan to me. A question dancing in his fire-lit eyes. Guilt presses in, crowding my already swarming emotions. Does Asher think there's something between Declan and I? I watch as Asher chugs whatever's left in his cup before tossing it into the soaring fire and walking away, leaving Nerissa mid-sentence. The beautiful fae doesn't waste any time pulling her attention back to Gabriel, who also appears confused about his friend's departure.

At my side, my hand jerks as Asher walks away. I want to correct him. To correct all of this. Us. I want to touch him. Hold him. I want what we no longer have. My chest is heavy with the weight of everything pressing within the walls of my ribs. Lead fills my lungs with each labored breath.

I bit my lip hard to surface pain that isn't related to my emotions.

Declan takes a step closer to me, clearly watching Asher as well. "You're thinking too much, love," he says against my hair.

I sway slowly against Declan's chest, the beat of the drums flowing through me. I swallow down the last of the alcohol in my cup. It's empty again. It's one of many I've finished. Luca continues to hand drinks to me and Declan continues to help me balance on my own two feet. Neither of them mentions Nerissa, Gabriel or Asher but I know they're still here.

Occasionally I can hear Nerissa's intrusive giggle linger into the night, grating against the melody of the drums. But every time I hear her, Luca pulls me farther into the crowd. The three of us have danced nonstop for the last hour.

I usually don't dance. Especially with Declan and especially when I know Lord Raske can see me with someone who is not his son. But tonight I don't care. Or should I say the abundance of alcohol drowning my system won't allow me to care.

Declan's fingers dig into my hips to hold me up and he pulls me closer against his chest as I sway to the music and I rest my head back on him. My head feels so weighted. The mass of people doesn't allow any air to flow over our sweaty bodies but Luca hands me another drink to cool me down a little. It doesn't seem to help.

Cracking my heavy eyes open, I give a lazy smile, she tilts her cup up at me, sloshing the drink over the edges of the cup and smiles back at me. She so rarely smiles, the gesture reminds me of how unearthly beautiful she is. Almost approachable even.

I feel Declan's head lean against my own as his fingers rise over the top of my dark jeans and brush lightly against my damp skin. Something tugs at my mind as he starts brushing a circle pattern over my bare hips with his fingertips. The feeling is hypnotic but I start to pull away out of reflex.

As I lean out of his grasp, I collide with something hard. I push my hands out in front of me, my fingers arching against solid muscle.

Opening my eyes, I find I'm face to face with Asher. His bare chest rises and falls visibly, his dark jeans almost disappear into the night, aside from the glint of the new Crimson Sword at his side. His skin is now clean, mud and sweat no longer cling to his body as it did when I laid eyes on him hours ago but without the dirt, the deep white lines of scars etching his flesh are easily seen.

The muscle is strung tight beneath my fingers. My drowsy eyes make their way slowly up the touchable lines of his chest, and meet his steely gaze. He looks down at me, his brows pulled low and his jaw strung with anger, twitching beneath the surface. He searches my face like a book that has no translation. My hazy mind offers nothing to him.

He takes his eyes off me for a moment to look up at Declan who stands a step behind me. The firelight reflects in Asher's crystal eyes, highlighting his fury.

"Why don't you go get some water?" Asher says softly, meeting my eyes again, hesitantly touching the hook of my arm. His fingers feel like a shock of electricity against my skin, bringing me to life after a year of numbness.

My palms have flattened against his chest now, making themselves at home in the divine crevices of his perfect body. My mind flutters to keep up with its surroundings. I fight to think rationally but I'm too tired to complete the effort. Besides, Asher's here. He's looking, speaking and touching me. Why find rationality when it isn't needed? Nothing needs to be rationed. I need this. In an abundance.

Wait, what?

He's still waiting for me to reply, for me to respond, I think. I smile up at his beautiful face, the only reply my mind allows me. An ache settles into my chest. Has he always been this good looking? How could my memory forget the light flecks of crystal amongst the gray in his eyes? My fingers push lightly against his pecs before tracing down the lines of his hard stomach, my index finger drifting off course to trail the length of the smooth scar, which matches my own, against his ribs. His muscles tense beneath my touch.

How has he gotten even sexier since the last time we touched?

My fingers are still traveling when he stops my hands at his lean waist. He's still breathing heavy but his expression is no longer filled with anger. *Why was he angry? Why was I angry?* Confusion crosses my face just as a look of pain fills his.

"Do you want Luca to take you back to your bed?" he whispers for only me to hear.

A tingle feathers over my skin as his breath sweeps over my warm neck.

My eyes fall shut. Sleep. Yes. Nothing has sounded more fantastic in all my life.

Nodding up at him, I watch him call over his shoulder and speak with Luca. They talk in slow motion for what feels like an eternity, but I don't mind. I could listen to his husky voice for hours, even if his words aren't registering in my thoughts. My fingers flex back and forth against the hard muscles of his abdomen. He holds my wrists lightly in his hands, like a puppeteer with a wandering puppet.

Their conversation of making sure 'Fallon has enough water to drink and isn't left alone tonight' is dragging on. My head grows heavy so I lean into him, resting my forehead against his chest. I breathe him in, a familiar scent of dirt, woods, and soap fill my nose.

"Luca's going to take you to bed now, Fallon." A dense pause settles into his whisper. He says my name like it's heavy in his mouth. "Be careful who you trust."

He pauses again like he's thinking through every word he speaks. Apprehension flits through my mind. *Should I be wary of the mystics here?*

"She's taken care of herself for almost a year now." Declan's angry and muffled voice cuts him off. I lift my head with concentrated effort to look over my shoulder at him and to better hear him. "Don't come ruin her fun because you found time to remember you cared about her."

Flickering rage ignites in his eyes as Asher glares at Declan from over my head. He slowly lowers my hands from him, disengaging our bodies. My hands are clammy at my sides without him and I put all my effort into following the conversation that swirls around me, reaching to catch the words that are too high above me to touch.

The people around us have stopped dancing and talking and now watch our every move. I suddenly want to be them. For the first time in my life, I want to see what others see when they look at me—on the outside looking in.

Luca takes my hand and pulls me from between the two hybrids. We stand a couple feet from them. She pulls at my hand like we might sneak off, but I refuse to leave. The cloud in my mind lifts slightly. Declan's words flow through my head on repeat. I, too, am intrigued in how Asher might respond.

"I didn't forget her," Asher says, his brow lowering in rage. He opens his mouth to explain further.

"Don't worry, because she finally forgot you," Declan says in a slow and low voice, cutting him off. Asher turns away from him like he might walk away entirely, shaking his head in annoyance but Declan takes a step closer to Asher. "I helped her forget you," he adds with taunting confidence, a smirk lighting his eyes as he licks his lips.

The muscles in Asher's arm tic. He never looks away from Declan. A few mystics glance my way questioningly, but I don't acknowledge them. The air is sucked out of my lungs at Declan's confession.

That's a lie! An exaggeration and an embarrassing confession that isn't his to confess. You can't speak for someone, even if they refuse to speak for themselves.

A second passes between them. The relentless drums have finally stopped pounding, realizing there's new entertainment tonight.

Asher searches Declan's eyes, calculating. I want to scream that it isn't true, to reassure him somehow but my tongue is thick in my mouth.

I can see Asher swallow hard, his Adam's apple bobbing, before looking around at the large crowd watching them. His eyes flash to Gabriel's, who stands across from me with his head held high to watch every move Declan makes.

Asher leans closer to Declan, his voice just above a whisper. "If you touch her again, I'll end your little royal life you've been playing at here." A sneering smile touches his lips. "The only thing you helped her forget is that there's probably a reason society keeps throwing away trash like you."

Declan's jaw tics and in a flash his fist is against Asher's face. I gasp at the sight of blood that gushes from his mouth, startled by the cracking sound that fills the air. Asher tenses but then laughs as the blood trickles down his chin and throat.

"Finally, a fucking reaction I was expecting in this place," Asher says, wiping the back of his hand against his bloody mouth, flinging the blood from his hand to the dirt.

Declan's posture changes, feet apart, fists clenched the way he has countless times during our training. Asher paces a small circle in front of him, working his jaw back and forth, a twisting smile lingering on his bloody lips.

Kaino pushes his way through the mass of people, the crowd bowing around the commander. Asher nods to him in acknowledgment, a seemingly pleasant gesture between friends. Kaino doesn't acknowledge the greeting, nor does he come between the two. It isn't the Wanderer's way. If confrontation occurs, it'll be settled immediately and never spoke of again. It will not be a reoccurring event.

Asher finally stops his short circular pacing and walks predatorily back to Declan. Declan stands on edge. His mind clearly working to calculate Asher's next move.

Standing face-to-face with one another it's strange to think I found any similarity between them. Asher's lean frame has become wrapped in muscle, still the beautiful hybrid I met over a year ago but stronger and angrier than he once was. I guess I am as well. It's what heartbreak does to a person. It makes you angry, but it also makes you stronger than you ever thought you could be.

Asher gives Declan another sadistically warm smile. Gently, he raises his palm to the side of Declan's face. Declan's eyes follow the slow, calm movement. Asher pats his hand against Declan's jaw the way a proud father would his son.

"When I said never to touch her again," Asher's eyes are lit red against the flames of the fire, his bloody smile never faltering as his low voice travels through the crowd. "That goes for me, too." He taps his palm one last time against Declan's jaw before shoving Declan's face down and slamming his other fist into the side of Declan's head. It happens so fast I barely track the movement at all.

I watch in horror as the side of Declan's face collides with Asher's fist, the sound of bone cracking fills the silence. The power in which Asher shoves Declan's face and the force of his fist connecting knocks Declan out immediately.

My stomach rolls and threatens to release all the alcohol I've dumped into it over the last couple hours. Asher lifts his eyes from Declan's motionless body on the ground to where I stand. The smile that was on display for Declan still mars his face but it's a sad, forced smile now.

He takes a couple of slow confident steps toward me. A guilty look fills his face as he searches my eyes as if expecting anger there. But I'm not angry. Declan had no right to say what he did. I wish it hadn't had happened at all but I'm not my friend's keeper.

Asher turns his head to spit, red tinged saliva covers the dirt. Blood still stains his throat, lips, and fists but when I look into his beautiful eyes, I'm filled with surprised happiness that he's still in there. My Asher. The one that cares if I think he's a monster or not.

"In case we never get formally introduced here," he holds out his bloody hand to me, his closeness spreading warmth into me. "My name's Asher Xavier."

EIGHT
A LIFE LONG LOST

Of course, I dream that night. It starts bittersweet this time. I dream of my mother. A nocturnal memory of my childhood. She's reading a fairy tale in my tiny bedroom back at our camp, the four walls closed tightly in on us. I'm curled up next to her as she tells tales of clever princesses and daring princes. The mother-daughter bond stirs questions of my father in my childlike mind. I push the thought of my father aside and snuggle closer to my mother. Happy just to have her here.

A confused aching grows heavy in my chest, a pain that I can't quite grasp. I smother the feeling out immediately and let my eyes drift closed as I listen to my mother's smooth voice calm me. So different from how we spoke just before she died.

She died.

The words float into my mind and my sad adolescent eyes jar open. But see nothing. Only darkness surrounds me. I feel around my blankets, but she's gone and I am alone. The warmth my mother's memory provided is also gone. A coldness bites into my skin and I struggle to burrow into the thin blankets.

"*Fallon*." A whisper echoes around the small room.

I still beneath the blanket and consider hiding my head from the eerie voice.

"*Fallon, follow me and you'll never suffer the feeling of loneliness for the rest of your days*," the harsh murmur says, crawling like a spider over my skin, weaving a web of whispers through my mind.

My heart starts to pound and I worry the voice can hear it in the silence. I steal a glance at the window Ayden climbed through countless times. The black sky outside is moonless and provides no lighting to soothe my fear.

Red eyes blink back at me within the dark and depthless room. Deep and unhelpful breaths fill my lungs as I heave for air, frantic heartbeats fill my chests. A sudden light appears across the red eyed monster within the room and a gasp is all I can manage when the thing looks back at me with a face identical to my own.

Unblinkingly I stare into the fiery eyes as I trace the sunken and deathly features of my own face. A chill runs over my body and I can feel the whisper crawl across my damp, clammy skin when it speaks again.

"*Fallon-*"

I flinch awake. My heart still hammering in my chest

as the whisper drifts through my mind over and over again.

A deep breath fills my lungs but my body is constricted. A strong arm is wrapped around me and a warm breath flutters across my sweating neck.

I'm surprised at first, my muscles tensing in place, but warm familiarity drifts through me.

Asher.

My heart calms, my breathing returns to normal in the safety of his arms.

I wonder how long he's been here. Luca walked me to my bunk after everything happened last night but I refused to let her babysit me. Even though I almost died climbing the rope up to my bed in my drunken state. It's still very dark out. Possibly only an hour or two has passed.

My mind has sobered since the celebration. Embarrassment washes over me at the memory of dancing in Declan's arms. Kaino saw me, which is mortifying enough, but the whole community saw me, too, I suppose. Even though I was annoyed at Asher's interest in Nerissa, I don't want him to think there is anything between Declan and I. I think further and remember touching Asher like a cat with a new ball of yarn and embarrassment flames my face.

How will I ever look anyone in the eye after last night?

"I'm sorry," Asher says in a remorseful voice against

my neck, fanning his breath over my body in an agonizingly slow sigh.

His words bring hesitation into my mind, taking me by surprise that he's awake. My body tingles against his breath. My heart racing back to life.

I wait for him to say more—what he's sorry for—but his words never come. He's sorry for tonight? For the last year? That he couldn't find me? That he couldn't save my mother?

"You're avoiding me."

His statement hangs in the air around us and I'm just not sure what to say. My chest feels heavy, overcrowded with too many emotions. Instead of speaking, I shift closer to him under my blanket, the boards sounding with my every move. The solace I find in his arms, in just being held, almost dissolves the pain that's building within me.

The wooden pallet barely supplies enough room for myself, so the space around us is limited. I'm amazed the frame holds both of our weight without crumbling to the ground below.

"You're different now." The simple statement seems to be clouded with confusion against his lips. "You're... sronger." His fingers trace my lean sides. "You're...who you've always been on the inside."

My chest aches being so close to him. My emotions are a storm of confusion. The pain I've held in for the past year is building within me and I release a shuddering breath into the night.

"A little quieter than I remember..."

"Where were you?" I ask almost accusingly, trying to catch my breath. Always trying to keep calm around Asher.

Seconds tick by, stolen in the silence by the night breeze. I start to wonder if he heard me at all. His arm that's folded comfortably over me drifts down to rest over my hip. Pulling me impossibly closer to him. A deep inhale is heard over my shoulder like he's about to relive a life long lost.

"After everything at the Burrow. After I told you to run, more veil came in. You," Another deep sigh, his warm breath falling down my spine. "You don't know how many nights I've lost sleep wondering if one of them found you. The veil infested the forest, Gabriel and I fled. He dragged me away, there was a moment I thought he was dragging a corpse along with him. We ran for days, never stopping. Weeks later, after I healed and we hadn't seen any sign of veil, I returned and tracked your trail the best I could but it was like you disappeared entirely."

The memory of stepping into the enchanted society, feeling like I somehow walked through a wall or shield, comes to mind. I did disappear and Asher wouldn't have found me unless he was brought here just like I was.

"I checked the Burrow, the cave, I even discreetly watched your camp for any sign of you. It was like the beautiful girl that constantly glared and watched me every day through the compound window never existed at all."

His arms tighten around me a bit more, hugging me to his chest.

"We hid in the mountains for months. That's where we removed his tracking device and chip." Where Gabriel lost his hand. In a place made of the only material strong enough to truly harm a hybrid.

Sorting through all of his information, I'm surprised they didn't run right into Luca during their searches for me.

"You've been in Pike's Peak this entire time?"

I feel him nod against my hair. He rests his head against my own.

They've been hiding in a mountain range that literally has their names on it—Pike's Peak—The Red Hills. All this time Luca's searched for him and he's been less than a day's hike away, living in the shadows of monsters. That's how he found me—found Luca I should say. The vampires helped him...

We're both quiet for a while. The strong thrum of his heartbeat against my back fills my chest with peace and his body, wrapped neatly around mine, keeps me warm against the light breeze. The fan of his breath against my neck is a constant reminder that he's all around me. Finally. After all this time.

I swallow the lump in my throat and water fills my eyes, threatening to spill over.

"I never stopped searching for you, despite my fears

that there would be nothing to find," he says against my messy hair.

His hands loosen comfortably around me and quiet tears slip down my cheeks at the thought of how many nights have passed without him holding me.

We lie in silence, his thumb brushing back and forth against my hip, the only sign that he's still awake. The bright stars that I've poured my heart out to night after night are shining down on us. Two friends lost, then found.

Friends. Is that what we still are? So much time has passed, yet lying in his arms feels as natural as breathing. So much has changed but this hasn't. We haven't felt like friends the last couple of days. I guess that's my own fault. I should tell Raske the truth. Kaino would be relieved.

I just can't lose Asher again. Even if I am ruining the future for other people, the people here, people like my camp family, people like Ayden. People who are forced into unions and solitude and jobs and lives they don't want. Is my own happiness not equal to theirs? My mother gave her life to see me happy. Could I be happy with Kaino? As happy as I am right now just lying next to this beautiful and broken hybrid?

"I should go," Asher says slowly but doesn't release me from his arms.

It's like he can sense my worry. My anxiety over something that is actually an easy choice for me.

"You should stay," I whisper back to him, keeping my eyes closed, my mind dancing between reality and sleep.

His chest heaves against my spine and he nestles his head closer to my neck. "Always so quietly confident," he says, his lips brushing my neck with every word, making my heart pound with the tiny wisps of air.

A smile forms against my lips at how easily persuaded he is.

NINE
WHAT DO YOU SEE

Luca seems drawn to Gabriel, I'm not sure why. He's the opposite of every male in this community. Maybe that's his appeal... The one armed, redheaded, blind hybrid that sticks out like a fish walking on land.

Through the throng of people, she leads us. They shift aside easily, making way for the two of us like tiny fearful row boats trying to avoid a hurricane. Luca's confidence is evident with every deliberate step she takes, in the way her shoulders are held, in the way that her hips sway as she walks. I realize where we were going the moment his voice carries over the crowd to us.

I don't know if my body will ever not recognize Asher's. Before I can even see him, my nerves are on edge, aware of his location like a magnet pulled to hard metal.

The crowd parts and Asher and Gabriel appear, standing against the tree line—outsiders looking in. No one gives them a second glance, but to my surprise, Kaino is there with them. Strangely enough, he's smiling—something I have never in my life seen the commander do. His smile is wide and wolf-like, white teeth fully on display. His hulking mass shakes at the shoulders from something that Asher says to him. The three of them laugh among themselves, amazing me even further when Asher pushes the commander's shoulder lightly, causing them all to laugh a bit more.

Their good mood falters and evaporates at the sight of us. Even Gabriel is aware of the change without seeing a thing.

"Good evening, Fallon, Luca," Kaino says, nodding politely to us, his personality turning bland the moment he sees us.

I smile at Kaino as Asher takes a drink from his cup, seemingly disinterested in both myself and Luca.

Kaino looks around like he might make his escape plan, like I'm suffocating him with my mere presence. I suppress an eye roll but Luca wastes no time joining the men, ignoring the awkward hum that surrounds us.

"You guys aren't dancing tonight?" she asks a bit sarcastically.

The idea of Kaino moving his hips, arms or feet for any purpose besides warfare seems unrealistic to me but I say nothing.

"I would but you haven't asked me yet," Gabriel says shrugging his shoulders at her.

An unsure smirk pulls at Luca's full lips as she eyes the hybrid, taken aback by his reply.

"Are you flirting with me, hybrid?" she asks, raising her head higher to meet his empty, white irises. A flicker of fiery curiosity ignites her eyes.

"Absolutely."

She steps closer to him. He doesn't move but I can see his breath falter slightly from her nearness, his wide chest hesitant to breathe around her. He stands tall, maybe an inch taller than Luca, his muscle tone is even and strong but not overbearing, more lengthy than bulky.

"Why?" she asks in a speculating tone, tilting her head at him, a soft line creasing her brows.

Why? Is she serious? She's a bit intimidating sure, but she's beautiful. Not that Gabriel knows that, I suppose.

"I'd be an idiot not to."

"How do you know I'm not hideous?" she says, studying him up and down, taking her time appraising the unseeing hybrid.

"Are you?"

He smiles at her, his teeth a brilliant slash of bright white and Luca leans into him at the sight of his kind smile.

A few moments pass between them, the beat of the drums counting each second.

"Of course not," she says confidently, pushing her bronze shoulders back straighter.

"I'd have to be more than blind not to know that, Beautiful."

Her usual glaring eyes and tight set lips break into a genuine smile at his words. Asher's eyebrows rise over his cup as he takes another long drink. He steals a glance at me and I can't help but smirk at the situation that's unfolding around us. Even Kaino isn't scowling... For the moment at least.

"Do you want to dance?" Gabriel asks, touching her arm lightly, his fingers lingering against her caramel skin.

She wastes no time, grabbing his hand and pulling him into the mass of people, disappearing from sight.

And I'm alone. With Kaino and Asher. The two mystics I avoid as if my life depends on it.

Perfect.

A silence stretches around us. Asher stands between us, his eyes drifting between Kaino and myself, waiting with a smirk to see which one of us will break first. It's a game to him, one he can easily win. His years of experience within the compound makes silence a friend to him.

Why did I come with Luca tonight?

I take a deep breath, my feet shifting nervously on their own accord.

"You look pretty tonight," Kaino says without emotion, waving a wide hand vaguely in my direction.

If he's being honest, I don't believe it. Kaino looks about attracted to me as a mouse is to a napping cat.

I roll my eyes at him as a laugh bubbles over Asher's lips.

Asher bumps his elbow into Kaino's arm. "You didn't tell me you were such a charmer. Got to give a guy warning before you use a line like that." Dimples mar his beautiful face as he winks at the stunned commander and casually walks away, brushing his chest against my arm as he weaves around me. His skin is against mine for mere seconds. The lost look in his eyes as he stares down at me breaks my heart, his eyes dip to my mouth as he swallows hard and in an instant he disappears into the crowd. Leaving me out of breath and alone with Prince Charming himself.

What a jerk.

Hours pass, the dawn threatening to overtake the skyline, and finally with reluctance, I decide I should go to bed. Night terrors have consumed my dreams for the past several nights. I wake sweating and shaking, wishing badly that Asher was there with me... If only I had the nerve to talk to him publicly, to find that closeness we once had.

I toss my empty paper cup into the fire and stand from my dusty spot on the hard ground. Kaino abandoned me long ago, Luca and Gabriel have kept me company off and on before disappearing into the night together.

As I leave, I see Declan sitting alone, his legs spread wide as he watches the celebration, his shoulders slouching low. I pause near his spot along the outskirts of the crowd, set far away from the others.

My heart slips a little, dipping for just an instant as my eyes meet his.

"Are you okay?" I ask, kneeling at his side.

A slashing white smile fills his face, a smile that I don't believe for an instant. "Perfect, thanks for asking."

I swallow, wondering why he alienates himself like this. Why did he say those things about us? I thought we were friends...

"Are we okay?" he finally asks, his eyes focusing on the empty cup in his hands.

I clasp his palm in mine, it's warm and calloused... Just like him.

"Yeah, we're okay," I say with a half-smile. "Could you help me get something? Supplies?" I ask, an idea crossing my mind.

"Of course. What do we need? I'll take care of it."

He sits forward now, his forearms resting on his thighs, coming closer to listen to my instructions.

Ripper makes his way from an enormous group of children, they all track the happy dog's every move. Out of everyone, Ripper might be the only one unaffected by what happened last year. The dog trails over to me on quiet paws, dancing at my side until I run my fingers through the short white hair at his temples.

"Can you get into the Department of Human Health?" I ask Declan in a conspiratorial whisper.

One of his blonde brows cocks high for just a moment before he nods slowly.

A real smile fills my face, excitement pushing

through me. Declan's lips quirk, a smile almost touching his lips as he sees my happiness.

I explain to him what the supplies are and what they might look like at the department, supplies that would normally never be wasted on lower class citizens. Supplies that Declan will have to steal from the government.

Declan agrees easily, not questioning why I need what I do, though I'm sure he knows. The special medical supplies are not something normal mystics need but will help one in particular.

There's nothing left to do. I make my way through the crowd and follow the shoreline to the mass of trees that my pallet resides in, Ripper follows me through the night. I don't make it into the forest though. There, standing at the shore is the walking image of the corpse I watched float away from me, never to be seen again. Until the Infinity witch stole her reflection.

My stomach sinks as her eyes meet mine. My mother smiles and the pain builds in my chest.

My feet move, walking toward her like I'm coming home after all this time. A low growl signals Ripper's dismissal. I stare after the little dog as he makes his way back to the children that love him. Some things never change. Ripper might always be wary of some of the mystics, but mortals have harmed him more than anyone...

The witch and I stand side by side, the breeze

shifting strands of her hair all around her worry-filled face.

"Sorrow so heavy I think it might cripple you fills your eyes whenever you look at me," she says as she glances down at me "What do you see when you look at me, child?"

She isn't anything like the first Infinity witch I met. She isn't lust filled or conniving. A feeling of wisdom and worry rolls off of her petite shoulders as she wraps her arms around herself.

I shake my head, not wanting to answer her.

"Answer my question and I'll answer one of yours."

I stare up at her, her face is so painful to look at.

"My mother, I see my mother." My voice shakes but I don't allow the emotion to grow. "Why are you different from the other witches?"

She smiles, a tired look that etches thin lines around my mother's beautiful face.

"Because I'm done. I wait for no one, other than death, my child. I spent centuries devouring love like a vulture to decaying meat. And I'm... exhausted. I want to be light again. Like youth before the dawn of adulthood, like sorrow before the tears, like the power of trust and the weakness of envy. I want to be full and I want to be empty all at the same time..."

My eyes widen at her confession.

"How long have you lived?"

"Sometimes life isn't about the number of years lived, but the amount of emotion felt." Her pale eyes appear lighter in the clear moonlight. She studies me for a moment, my mother's features smoothing into a sight of kindness. "In all of my life, I've never once had anyone look at me the way that hybrid looks at you."

I swallow hard and blink up at her. How does Asher look at me?

She lifts her arms and dithers for just a moment, unsure of herself, before wrapping her thin arms around me, embracing me.

"What do you wish you would have told your mother?" she asks, as I cling to her, wishing I would just push this strange witch away but also never wanting to let go.

My breath catches, coming out uneven and harsh, as my lungs grow tight. "I-" I gasp in an attempt at finding my breath again. "I wish I would have said thank you."

She knew that I loved her. So much. But she didn't know how much I appreciate all that she did for me. She lost her life to give me a better one.

"You're welcome, Fallon."

TEN
THE PRESIDENT

The much-awaited Treaty Celebration is finally here. My stomach fills with dread at the thought of meeting the representatives. Luca's swift fingers tangle my waves into a simple knot, a few loose tendrils curl around my face, threatening to cling to my lips.

"The mortals don't have much taste but I think this should do," she tells me, her mouth twisting in a look of uncertainty as she eyes my hair.

"That sounded incredibly close to an insult," I say as my eyes narrow on my friend.

She smirks at me, the dim light catching her golden-like eyes as she appears lost in thought. Flipping her long maroon hair, she turns away, striding to the door in a few long steps.

"I'll meet you at the dinner in just a few minutes." She races from her hut without explanation, the thin door creaking shut behind her, leaving me staring after her.

That was odd. She seems to be in a bit of a hurry.

Raske's warning for the hybrids to stay out of sight tonight circle my mind. I wonder if she's helping them hide, if she's using it as an excuse to get closer to Gabriel.

I sigh and begin pulling on my dress for the evening. It isn't the Wanderer's normal attire. It's a black dress that falls to my mid-thigh with thick straps over my tan shoulders. The smooth material feels nice against my skin. It swishes around my thighs with each step I take, reminding me of how calming the simple fabric feels. It might help me with my nerves tonight.

The sound of the door shutting quietly is heard as I pull the dress over my thighs. My heart skips a beat as I hold the fabric to my chest, glancing over my shoulder my gaze collides with hungry eyes.

Asher clears his throat, brushing a hand through his messy hair as he hastily looks to the floor. "Sorry, I-" he stammers. The always assured hybrid can't seem to fill a sentence right now.

A shy smile pulls at my lips as I finish pulling on the black formal dress, the dress hugs my shoulders, barely revealing any skin in the front. The length of my spine is displayed with the low dip of the material in the back.

I face him when I'm fully clothed and he finally meets my eyes again, a sweet smile fills his face.

"I just wanted to see you before everyone got here," he tells me in a quiet voice.

He crosses the small room until he's just a foot from

me. His eyes trail over my skin, making a flush creep over my neck and face from the appraising look he's giving me.

"You're beautiful, Fallon," His voice is barely a rasp. "You're always beautiful."

I lean into him, unable to help the pull I feel when he's around and he wraps his arms around me in an instant. The beat of his heart fills my mind as he just lets me relax against his body. The anxiousness I felt moments ago isn't there anymore. I breathe in his warm scent as I nestle into his chest, my hands slipping around his trim waist, brushing over the hilt of the Crimson Sword as I go.

"I wanted to tell you to be careful tonight," he says against my hair.

Just like that, the calmness is pulled out from under me.

"Why?"

"I know what Raske intends for you." I shift until I'm looking up into his concerned eyes, a thin line creases between his brows. "I—I'm not going to—I don't want to talk about that." He closes his eyes and takes a deep breath before meeting my confused gaze again. "The government isn't just going to let him join the races. Be careful of your words. I wish I could tell Raske to be careful, as well. Don't put yourself in danger for him."

I swallow hard, knowing he's right. I've thought the same thing hundreds of times. I nod and lower my head back to his chest, hoping to find the comfort I had. But it's gone. A nervousness churns my stomach as he holds me close. I close my eyes against the growing dread that is now heavier than it was before.

I won't have Asher to lean on tonight.

At Luca's side, I sit, shifting restlessly in the hard chair that bites into my spine. The tent has been lowered, we'll eat beneath the shining stars tonight.

In silence. The ever present drums that accompany the celebrations are not beating through the wind tonight.

"Nervous?" Luca asks, quirking her eyebrow at me as I wiggle in my chair once more.

I bite my lip and nod. No one has joined us yet aside from Kaino and Shane, who sit side by side. The two don't speak or even acknowledge each other. Stiff posture fills their broad shoulders as they stare off into nothingness. They're odd, almost intentionally ignoring one another.

The need to turn away from them fills me as their uncomfortableness begins to seep into me. I glance toward the head of the table as Raske and a group of five walks toward us. They take in the sights of our camp, admiring the display of mystics as if they're a rare commodity instead of a shunned community.

Kaino stands, meeting his father's eyes, his hands held neatly behind his back.

"President Docile, you remember my son, Kaino,"

Raske says, waving an arm proudly to the warrior standing before them.

I find it strange that Luca isn't mentioned once. The daughter of the lord apparently isn't of importance.

The president is an even stranger sight. Dressed in all black from head to toe, a shrouding black veil covers the woman's face. Soft blonde hair slips out beneath the curtain, revealing a single feature to us. The uneasiness flips in my stomach again at the hidden sight of the president.

Why is she dressed like that? Is that the way everyone dresses in Congress? Has she lost someone she loves? An appearance of mourning symbolized in her attire...

I glance toward Luca but she doesn't return my confusion. A charming smile is plastered across her lips as she gazes at the president.

"Please take a seat. Dinner will be served shortly," Raske tells them in a formal voice that I have never heard before.

I sit on my hands to keep myself still as the group of representatives begin taking their seats across from us.

A man pulls out the seat across from me. As he's about to take his seat his dark eyes meet mine, stopping him in his tracks.

"Ayden?" I stand, an astonished smile filling my face, the strange president and my anxious nerves all but forgotten.

"What are you doing here?" he asks, his eyes tracing

every curve of my body, seemingly searching for injury where there is none. "Are you all right?"

He comes around the table, holding me by the arms as he does his assessment at a closer stance. An enormous and filling happiness floats through me, making me unable to contain the smile on my face.

"I'm fine, Ayden."

Everyone has stopped what they're doing and is now watching us intently. Kaino and Shane have even snapped out of it enough to realize something is happening, their eyes moving from me to the representative that has me clasped in his hands.

"I thought I'd never see you again," he says in a quiet breath.

"Ayden, come sit down. We'll have plenty of time to reminisce throughout the evening," a man says from across the table.

Seated next to President Docile is a man who was once my mentor. I blink a few times, trying to grasp on to all the familiar faces of my past that are now here in this community of mystics. Ayden gives me another long look before taking his seat across from me, next to my mentor.

"I'm happy you're all right, Fallon." Straight white teeth fill my mentors smile as he beams at me. A black button down shirt is crisp against his chest and he smooths it relentlessly in an almost nervous fashion. More gray hair streaks his dark brown hair than I remember, but his eyes are still kind and caring. "I helped Ayden place flyers through the villages. He was worried about his friend... Everyone was worried. We'll have to update them of your safety to ease their minds."

It's a lie; one I can effortlessly spot. They won't take time to update the surrounding communities. He continues to brush his palm down the imaginary wrinkles of his shirt.

"Lorde Raske, this is my friend from my village, Ayden, and this is my mentor, Michael. He helped structure my future from a very young age, focusing on my strengths and weakness to find my perfect place in society." The word future circles my mind. What a waste all that time was. My future isn't anything like the plans the government mapped out for me.

Lord Raske nods to the two men, his smile genuine as he speaks. "It's good that Fallon has so many people that care about her."

My heart pounds, picking up speed as I realize I haven't had these people with me. I've been mostly alone for the past year. A weak smile pulls across my lips, not reaching high enough to touch my eyes or my mood.

A fae in his early twenties, short blonde hair combed neatly back, his shirt tucked perfectly into pressed white slacks walks toward us. He places a heaping plate of green beans down in the center of the table, leaning closely over Kaino's side, making the warrior fidget in his seat from the fae's nearness. The wolf's muscly arms shift at an odd angle to dodge the fae's thigh that brushes against Kaino's chair.

Other caterers join us, placing food on the table like

decorations. The warm smell greets me, reminding me of how hungry I really am, distracting me for just a moment from the guests seated across from me.

"Please, eat," Raske says to us all with an excited smile.

Everyone begins filling their plates as instructed, minimal words are exchanged, a feeling of uneasiness begins to thrum through the silence. The president appears to look over the mounds of appetizing food piled around the table but doesn't make a single move to touch any of it. Pale hands are clasped before her as she sits with immaculate posture.

Luca passes me a look, her elbow leaning heavily on the tabletop, her lips quirking in a smile like she'd rather be anywhere but here.

"How have you been?" Ayden asks, his plate void of any food as he watches me shovel in a heaping spoon full of mashed potatoes.

"I've been really good. It's amazing here. Freeing." I clamp my mouth shut on the last word. *Should I have said that?*

I glance to Raske and the president but they're speaking quietly among themselves, ignoring me entirely.

I relax and give Ayden a small smile.

"How's Congress? You seem to be doing so well," I say and my stomach dips as I realize how formal my tone sounds. Not spoken with a lifetime of friendship but with... polite unattached words. Ayden and I are barely friends at all now.

I don't really know the man seated across from me at all...

I take a sip from my glass and my throat constricts as the ice water tilts from the cup. I lower the drink as I cough, fumeless and pure water is all that I taste. Just water. Glancing into Luca's drink I confirm that she, too, isn't drinking alcohol. No alcohol tonight? The one night that I need it, the Wanderers are suddenly a sober community.

Great.

Luca quirks a delicate brow at me as she takes a bite of her steamed broccoli. I shake my head at her and draw my attention back to Ayden.

"It's good. It's really good," he says, but his look doesn't reflect this. Sadness touches his russet eyes, a frown threatening the smile that's tilting his lips.

I stare at him for a few moments, the sweet, gangly boy I grew up with is no longer present. We're both older now, aged by society in different ways. He's as happy as he always knew he would be; miserable is an understatement.

"I missed you," I finally say, the words nothing more than a whispered revelation.

The smile that's in place against his lips pulls a little higher, almost genuine. "I—" He pauses, glancing to Michael who looks quickly away from us, pretending to be enthralled with the baked chicken on his plate. "I missed you, too," Ayden says, his solemn eyes drifting away from mine, staring at his hands that are neatly folded in his lap.

My brows lower as my stomach sinks.

We're not at all the friends we once were.

"Tell me, do you work with your mentor, Ayden?" Raske asks, raising his head high to look down the table at the man seated across from me.

Ayden glances to Michael as if the man might guide him in his response. Michael shifts in his chair, his eyes not meeting anyone else's, like his personality is shrinking away from us by the second with uncouth movements.

"No, I didn't have a mentor."

"You didn't have a mentor?" I repeat, bringing my attention back to him, my spoon held at mouth level, but forgotten.

How did I not know this about my friend?

"No, you were the only person I knew that had a mentor," Ayden says before taking a big drink of water and busying himself by filling his plate finally.

Lord Raske's dark button-like eyes shift from Ayden to Michael a few times before he lowers his attention back to the dune of hot food in front of him.

I study Michael for a few moments, the sweat that adorns his creased brow, his thin lips that he licks repeatedly between messy bites. The overall nervous energy that's pouring off of him. The wolf seated across from him assesses these details, as well.

Kaino's slow traveling eyes seemingly catch every minor

thing Michael does, almost as if he's storing the actions away in a large file within his mind. Kaino holds his hands in front of him, braced on his elbows against the table. Massive hands are clasped in front of him, one fist is held in the other while he sits quietly watching the representative eat.

When did Michael become someone to be monitored? He was my friend all my life. Or was he?

Shane bumps his arm against Kaino's, sending him a questioning look before returning to the mound of food before him, drawing Kaino's attention away from the suspicious human.

Dinner passes slowly, dread and sadness and impatience is forming with every hour that we sit at the table. Raske insisted on a private meeting with the president that has taken longer than I thought it might. I know what they're discussing and I want to run and hide before the two of them have a chance to return.

I stand from my seat, Michael, Ayden and the other two representatives look up at me. Kaino and Shane whisper quietly among themselves, while Luca subtly etches her blade into the side of the wooden table. She has a nice divot carved into it and doesn't seem to be drawing attention to herself as she whittles away.

"Sorry, I haven't been feeling well. It was very nice meeting you all..." I pause as everyone stops to stare at me. I begin to get the feeling that leaving isn't an option just yet. "Please tell the president it was an honor to meet her. Sail safely on your journey home." More surprised attention pins me to my spot.

I give a hesitant smile that probably resembles fumbling nervousness rather than happiness.

"Let me walk you to your hut," Ayden says, pushing out his chair in an instant, not looking back at the other representatives that stare wildly at him.

Michael's face is set into a look of panic, a look that almost makes me hesitant to leave. "It was nice seeing you again, Michael," I tell him in an unsure voice as I walk toward the tree line.

He nods at me absentmindedly before turning back to his empty plate.

It was strange seeing him again, he was so kind to me when I was in school and now Michael just seems... distant. As if his thoughts are being pulled in a million directions and he can't think through any of them long enough to get a word out.

Ayden and I walk at a snail's pace back to my bunk, I don't tell him that I don't sleep in the huts. My reclusive life is no one's business but my own. I keep waiting for him to say something. Anything. Silence is the only thing between us.

I stop at the tree that houses my bunk, he turns on his heels when he realizes I'm not at his side. Dark eyes stare down at me, too close for comfort, eyes that are filled with the thoughts of a man I no longer recognize. He looks at me with confusion marring his smooth features.

His long legs are just inches from mine, his lips parted, lips that once kissed mine with so much devotion

I thought he'd always own a part of my heart. It was never his to own though...

"I—I've thought about you every day." His hand moves at his side as if he might reach out to me but he closes his fist tightly and lowers it at his side. His eyes leave mine as he studies the leaves between our feet, his pristinely shined shoes offsetting my dusty sandals. "Did he hurt you?"

"No, he helped me."

His eyes snap to me once more, his lips part as a breath shakes out, a laugh threatening his voice. "He helped you? Tearing you away from your friends and family. He helped you?"

A long breath fills my lungs, my eyes closing briefly as I try to think of how to explain this to someone that no longer knows me. Someone that couldn't even understand my life if I wrote it out in black and white.

"I can't explain it, Ayden, but just think about your life and mine. Are you happy? In the life that you live, are you happy? Because I'm the happiest I've been in all my life."

It's odd to think about, my life here is strange, a bit lonely at times, but it's mine. If I wanted to leave tomorrow I could. If I want one child or a hundred no one would question it. If I wanted to spend the rest of my life alone it would be entirely my decision.

And if I wanted to spend my days with one beautifully lethal hybrid vampire... I could.

"Fallon, you left before I could properly meet you,"

President Docile's smooth and pleasant voice floats over my shoulder.

Her face is still curtained by the thin black veil that shields her features from me. My fingers itch to push the fabric aside but I force myself to keep my hands at my sides.

Her thin body sways closer to me, grace fills her every move, so out of place in the wild Wandering community.

"Mr. Raske has told me so much about you. I just had to meet the human girl that has become so taken with Kaino. He is a charming boy, isn't he?"

Her statement catches me off guard and my mouth hangs open, no words or even a breath slips over my lips. My brows rise high and I find myself looking to Lord Raske or Kaino or anyone of the representatives standing behind the president. No one says a word.

I feel Ayden's eyes on me, unspoken questions fill the silence.

"Yes, he's very..." I pause, grasping for a word to accurately describe Kaino in a positive light. "Protective," I finally sputter.

Thick, dark lashes fan across Kaino's cheeks as he cringes from my description. I see the sigh he releases from his wide chest but he remains quiet.

Raske smiles at me, nodding, pleased with my kind words. The president's veil shakes as she seems to nod at me. Her thin, pale hands are held neatly in front of her, perfect posture has her sharp shoulders strung tight.

"How nice. Perhaps we will have to revisit the

Wanderers in the near future." The strange woman turns toward Michael who zeroes his attention in on the woman, taking a step closer to her, ready for her every demand. She raises a hand to his shoulder, resting it there against the pressed white shirt. "Let's be sure to... check in on the progress of this couple and their community very soon."

Michael makes note of her words, scribbling quickly across a small white pad of paper.

She pauses, her shrouded, faceless body appearing to stare at me for a moment longer before she sweeps away, shifting dead leaves and dust in her wake.

Lord Raske, Kaino and the other representatives trail after her. Except for Michael.

My mentor's brows crease as he looks down at me, his lips pinched into a thin, almost nonexistent line. "Be careful, Fallon. Of who you trust, and of who you love. Just"- He swallows hard, a minimal amount of stubble coats his throat and jaw line. He glances over his shoulder at the group of mortals and mystics that are fading into the shadows of the night. "Just don't... Don't marry that wolf, Fallon. Nothing good will come from uniting our races. Nothing." He turns before I can even reply, before I can even fully consider his strange words.

He runs after his president, wading through the thick trees and shadows until he disappears entirely.

"What right does he have to tell me who to be with?" I ask more to myself than to Ayden.

I glance up at him and find him staring at me. A deep

line etched between his brows as he glares down at the person he once called a friend.

Ayden's always hated the mystics. More than most humans. He might hate me, too, now.

"Because he's your father, Fallon."

ELEVEN
LIKE A MEMORY

The representatives left early but I laid awake thinking about what Ayden said to me long into the quiet night. I didn't sleep for more than an hour. After the shock wore off my tired eyes finally drifted to sleep. I awoke soon after with the voices circling my mind again, gnawing at my consciousness until my eyes flew open.

Leaving me to dwell on my life.

Ayden wouldn't lie to me. I don't think he'll ever be dishonest with me no matter how much he may hate me now. It makes sense that Michael would be my father really. He's been a part of my life since I can remember. Visiting me twice a year during school to make sure I focused on all the right subjects, he helped me find my talents, he arranged my union... I guess in a strange way he's the reason I am where I am in life.

A yawn pulls at my tired body as I blink hard and try to find the positivity that this day holds.

Hours later I lead Gabriel into the empty clinic, Asher and Luca follow close behind. Gabriel's eyes shift around, his head tilting, listening for any kind of insight his other senses might offer him. Suddenly, I'm aware of what he might sense; the way the sun filters off into the humid room, the way my boots softly thud against the tile, the way we're all holding our breath as we watch the blind hybrid stare aimlessly around the clinic.

"We're inside?" He pauses just within the doorway, his lean frame blocking out the bright rays of sunlight.

Asher and Luca trail in after Gabriel taking up the majority of the space within the small white room. I walk to the back where the package was left for me, excitement simmers in my chest and soaks through my limbs at the idea of what I'm about to do.

"You know if you have some kind of attack planned, you can't really do any more damage than there already is," Gabriel says, his voice echoing through the empty room.

I smirk at his words. He stands leaning against the wall, almost hesitant to proceed any farther into the room. His fiery red hair has been trimmed and shaven close at the sides, a much cleaner look than when he first arrived, he looks a little less broken, too.

"Listen, it's not every day a girl approaches you with a surprise. Maybe you should hear her out first," Asher says to him, smirking at me out of the corner of his eye.

My face warms at his words and I can't help but smile. Luca assesses Gabriel discreetly. Something she does to everyone, I've noticed. This time it's different. Her eyes travel over the hybrid, looking not at his stature or motives but really at him. At his body, at his wide shoulders and slim waist and everywhere in between.

I arch an accusing eyebrow at her and she shrugs, her shoulders rising minimally when she realizes she's been caught. She offers a small smirk before turning away from us to look around the room at the few pictures that decorate the walls.

The pictures are old, from ages ago. From a time when medicine wasn't just for the dying but for the sick and the elderly. It was all but wasted on such minor issues it makes me sick to my stomach. Imagine what a plethora of medicine like that could do for the people back at camp.

"So, what is it? You going to put a band aid on this limb or what? Listen, I've tried and the whole band-aid thing doesn't make it much better. Prettier; but not better," Gabriel says with a half-smile.

"Do you always talk this much?" Luca asks, her back still turned to us, her fingers brushing over a framed picture of a doctor helping an elderly lady with a walker.

"Only when I know people are listening," Gabriel replies, his body shifting toward her voice.

Ignoring their banter, I start pulling the wrappings from around the item within the box, my excitement increasing with every piece of tissue and plastic I pull away.

Asher grows serious as he watches me. Our eyes meet

for just a moment before I look away from him. A strange fluttering awakens within my chest, a feeling that he's given me since the day we met.

Luca turns to me just as I pull away the last of the plastic wrapper from around my gift to Gabriel. Her surprised intake of breath is audible and Asher's eyes widen as he stares down at it.

The room is entirely silent. The item is smooth against my palms, a symbol of something clean, new and full of hope.

"How the hell did you get that?" Asher asks, his eyes never leaving it.

I pause not wanting to discuss that topic. I busy myself picking up the paper and plastic that surround my feet and stuffing them into the box.

"Declan got this for you, didn't he?"

"What is it? Can someone spare a moment for the blind? Anyone?"

Asher's jaw clenches, a look of vacantness filling his smooth features when I offer him a tense smile in reply. I ignore him, not letting the excitement slip away from me. He doesn't trust Declan but he doesn't know him either.

I stand and walk slowly toward Gabriel. My palm slips over his arm, he tenses under my touch. His limb is smooth, the tissue nicely healed. A good sign. Asher was careful with his work even if it was rushed.

"You know if you wanted to get me alone, I'd be happy to tell Asher to get lost," Gabriel whispers loudly to me, leaning his body intentionally closer.

He's nervous, I can hear it in his uneven voice even if his face doesn't show it. Hybrids don't seem short on confidence even if they can't see the world around them.

"Don't ruin this, Gabe," Asher says laughing, pushing his friend's shoulder lightly.

I settle the metal carefully against his limb. It aligns perfectly. The strap slips over his wrist, I fasten it a little tight, making sure everything is in place before activating it. It hums quietly to life at his new metal fingertips.

"What – What the hell is this?" he asks harshly as the tendons in his arms shift beneath the skin and the fingers wave slowly.

"It's a bionic prosthetic," I say quietly, my eyes mystified by the fluid bionic actions.

I've never had access to anything so medically perfect. Things like this aren't made for lower class mortals. It especially isn't made for a mystic. Just like Ky, we've fumbled around with supplies that aren't making anyone's lives any easier. Ky was lucky to have been approved for a prosthetic at all. If Gabriel was mortal they'd never waste a prosthetic on him. Not when he still has one other good hand.

Flawlessly it moves without any tics or pauses, as if the hybrid was born with it. My heart booms and an enormous smile consumes me with a feeling of achievement. Without sound or struggle, he waves his new hand at us. He brings his other hand up to meet it and steeples his fingers together, the hard metal pressing against smooth flesh.

Asher's dimples appear as a wide smile slowly crosses his face, all thoughts of Declan are gone. I'm captivated by every small move he makes with it. When I look to Luca, I expect the same reaction to the bionic hand but she isn't looking at it at all. She's watching Gabriel's face, a small smile pulling at her parted lips.

"What's it feel like?" Asher asks, his silver eyes catching the glare off the sleek metal.

Gabriel touches the wall with his new hand, brushing over the concrete, his nimble fingers effortlessly open the blinds. Then he bends to unlace and re-lace his shoes with quick fluid gestures.

"It feels like a memory," he says, standing still now turning his hand back and forth before us all. "It feels simple and easy and taken for granted and," he pauses, his eyebrows arching, "normal."

A mixture of pain and happiness pushes into my chest, Asher reaches out without looking at me and takes my hand in his, his warm fingers fitting perfectly against mine. I can feel his simple happiness spread into me from the small touch.

"So, you like it?" I ask, trying to contain the smile that threatens to consume my whole face.

"It *is* better than a band-aid."

He swallows and looks away from us, his white eyes shining in the sunlight that he let in from the open blinds.

It's that easy. The government has this technology laying around and millions of people all over the world need it, but only the *deserving* receive it.

Gabriel deserves it and more. He's survived so much. So much that he's no longer living. Just surviving. Taking each day with the expectancy that it might be his last. He smiles freely, he laughs loudly, he talks candidly. Because he knows there isn't time to wait. Time doesn't wait. It presses you forward whether you're ready or not.

Gabriel's been there, to the place time took him against his will. He lost so much.

But I can give him this. The best medical technology the world has to offer and it's now at his fingertips, a gift of power and love offered between a human and hybrid.

"What you did today, for Gabriel. That was amazing," Asher says, breathing me in as his hands hold me tightly to his chest.

His head rests in the nook of my neck, his breath fanning down my back, sending a tingling sensation across my skin. Another perfect night in his arms.

"Just be prepared for an endless stream of *Fallon lent me a hand once* jokes." I laugh quietly at his words. "No seriously, I already heard it three times today and he doesn't show any signs of stopping anytime soon."

"I hope he doesn't. I like his jokes."

"Oh, for the love of everything good in the world, please do not tell him that."

A smile consumes my face, a happiness I feel deep in my chest... in my heart. Everything is so easy now. Asher and I, even if we are only ever friends to one another, we click. He's like soil and I'm a seed and with him holding me together, supporting me, something beautiful grows. Something undamaged and untouched by society.

His arms tighten around me, pulling me flush against his chest. Warmth spreads into me, his scent filling the air around me. My eyes drift involuntarily and a peaceful sleep falls over me.

For a few hours at least.

Before the voices return, clawing into my subconscious and settling in there.

TWELVE
WHAT I WANTED

The Infinity witch's words have been on my mind relentlessly lately. Every time I catch Asher looking at me, I can't help but dissect his appearance, trying to see what he holds in his eyes when he watches me.

But I don't see it. He's the same handsome hybrid he's always been.

Except right now.

He nods his head, motioning me to follow him into the shadows. He walks away, leaving Gabriel blankly staring after him. The redhead gives me a knowing smirk as I follow discreetly after Asher into the night.

The firelight and laughter is left far behind as I search blindly through the darkness for the one mystic I can't seem to stay away from.

I find him lying near the Emerald Ocean, an enormous cliff is just a few feet away from him. The moon is full tonight and seems to cast down on just him, highlighting his body against the dry, scorched land.

The sound of my steps are quiet, my boots falling softly with each careful step I take. He looks up at me as I stand over him, the moon directly behind me. A smile hesitates against his lips.

"Lie down with me." It isn't a question or a command. His voice is almost... unsure, like I might walk away from him at any moment.

I don't of course. I lie down, leaving a few inches of space between us until he drags my body against his, swooping me up into his arms in one quick motion. My head rests against his chest, my limbs not quite sure where they should go. Usually, he holds me and I don't have to question what I should do.

He lets a minute slip by with my hand held awkwardly above us before he takes it in his and rests it against his abdomen. His warm palm easing any nervousness I had felt just moments ago.

The endless starlight shines above us, lighting up the sky, keeping my attention off of the nerves that fill my restless body.

"Your heart's so loud," I finally say to fill the quietness as I listen to the strong beats within his chest.

A long breath is his only reply before he finally replies in a whisper, "That's because it beats for you."

My own heart flutters and a smile fills my face. "Have you waited an entire year to use that line?" I ask teasingly.

Laughter rumbles through his chest as he brushes his thumb back and forth against my hand.

"I've had a year to think about what I would say to you. I'm just getting started, baby."

The celebration is wildly heard within the night but for a few moments it's just him and I.

"Did you speak to the vampires?" I ask in a quiet voice, already knowing the answer to my question.

"I did." He shifts beneath me, not pulling away but moving with restlessness.

"What did they tell you? Did they tell you where I was?"

He clears his throat. "Don't ever go back there. They were not left here to help us, Fallon. They might be near dead, but they're more dangerous than they appear."

I nod, knowing he's right, but they still got me what I wanted.

Him.

THIRTEEN
MINE

THE BOARDS CREAK in protest under the movement of new weight behind me, interrupting another clawing nightmare. My eyes flutter open in the darkness, the shadowed forest greeting me, but I don't turn to him. He pulls himself up onto my pallet as quietly as possible, the boards whining, the woodlands silent in the presence of an age old predator. The warmth of his body sliding against mine wakes me in an instant.

Over the last couple of weeks, it's become our introduction to the hours of words to come. These hours are the most we ever speak to one another. The night eats up our words in the warm breeze, words that are lost to us by the following dawn. Passing each other as strangers during the day among the other Wanderers.

"How was your day?" he asks in a hushed tone, slipping his hand easily around my hip. The hard board bites into my side as his gentle fingertips caresses my other side.

His touch settles into my body. A chain reaction of warmth, tingling, and near lightheadedness flows through me.

"Uneventful," I reply, waiting for his next words, hanging on words unspoken. A feeling of intoxication spreads through me from our few minutes we've had together already.

His hand shifts slowly from my hip to my stomach, resting flat against my navel. His strength pulls me closer to his hard body. I feel his breath on my neck before he speaks.

"Kaino pulled me aside today." He leaves the statement hanging between us for a moment. "He asked if I knew you from somewhere. He said the two of us appeared to be conspiring and asked if there was anything he should worry about."

My body tenses against him. Kaino noticed us noticing each other? How is that possible? We barely speak in public. Not that it's a major deal. Raske seems to accept Asher and Gabriel and that's all that really matters. Would he still accept them if he realized my lack of interest in Kaino and my overwhelming interest in Asher?

Asher's long fingers start to massage and dance along my stomach.

"What did you say?"

His hand pauses for just a moment before restarting, his touch distracting me from the topic.

"Hmmm, what *did* I say?" His deep whisper vibrates against my back and into my chest. My eyes close, enjoying the feeling for just a moment.

"Don't tease, what did you tell him?" I ask in all seriousness.

A low laugh brushes against my hair, rumbling through me in a delicious and unique way. The feeling tumbles through my body and settles low in my stomach.

"I didn't break his heart, don't worry so much." His fingers travel down my stomach, lightly skimming my skin and playing with the top of my jeans. "Why? Would it bother you if I told your prince that I held you in my arms every night? That I wrap myself around you like I used to before." His voice is even quieter now but with more confidence, his warm breath whispering over my flesh. "That the only happiness I feel every day is the few hours I get when my hands are on your body. That the sharp breaths you take when I touch you are the only indication that you care for me at all."

I open my mouth to speak, his surprising confession startling me. But I don't know what to say. His hand stops toying with my body and pulls on my hip until I'm flat on my back, looking up at him leaning over me, the bright stars glistening behind him, once again the archangel within the heavens.

I breathe in the dry, salty air and take in his clean

scent. His crystal eyes search my face. His jaw strung tight, like the day I first laid eyes on him in the compound. He leans against one arm while his other drifts low over my hips, his fingers lightly digging into my skin.

"Are you jealous of Kaino?" I ask in a speculating whisper.

A small smile tugs at his serious face. His eyes narrow and his breathing accelerates just slightly. Just enough for me to notice in our close proximity.

"Kaino, no. Declan..." He pauses looking into my eyes for any signs I might give him.

I give him nothing.

"Maybe."

I smile shyly at his confession. I make him jealous? The idea of it flutters happiness through me and guilts me all at once. Asher's so perfect, even his imperfections are perfect to me. He's hurt, and our past has hurt me. We're both pained and jagged but together we're almost smooth again. Our fates have been mixed together so much it's strange that we are where we are right now. Side by jagged side. Together.

He has nothing to be jealous of. But a question still swarms my mind.

"Why not Kaino?"

He gives a deep and knowing laugh. It's loud in the silence and fills the forest, scattering a few birds from their quiet hiding spots. It breaks across his face and his rarely seen dimples even make an appearance. Why is that so funny? I understand Kaino may not be the most...

affectionate person towards almost anyone. But the idea of Kaino and I together is really this laughable to him?

My brows lower in annoyance and I shift slightly away from his warmth. There's limited space on the pallet but I still put the effort into disconnecting my body from his side.

"Hey, don't do that," he says playfully, still displaying the world's most annoyingly beautiful smile. He pulls me back to him and lowers his body closer to mine, his bare shoulder brushing against mine. "I didn't mean it like that. It's just," He pauses and looks away from me for a moment. He's considering his next words carefully. "There are a hundred reasons why I'm not jealous of the commander." He bites his lip to try to keep from smiling again. "But him placing that sexy hitch in your breath that I give you every night, isn't even a possibility."

My breath falters and I gasp when he lowers his strong body against me. Silver, questioning eyes search mine. His face is once again serious, all shadowed angles emphasized in white moonlight. His weight pushes against me deliciously and nothing has ever made me feel so... complete. His legs settle between mine and a feeling begins tingling through my stomach as my thighs clench tightly around his hips.

My hands drift up his body to his hard chest, the need to be closer soaring under my skin. He leans against one arm near my head as the other trails up my body from my hip, lightly traveling over my stomach, my ribs, my chest and collar bone, before cradling my neck. Clear eyes question mine, a look of uncertainty fill the depths of his gaze. He leans into me, our hair brushing. My heart pounds into his chest, communicating to him without words. The only sign language he ever taught me.

"So no, I'm not jealous of Kaino, because," he lowers his lips to mine, not quite touching, our warm breath mingling, "no one will ever take away what's mine again."

His lips brush mine, warm and slow. Then the world stops around us. Falling into nothingness. It's a gentle kiss. My heart flutters in my chest, softly against his hard body. My fingers release his shoulders and push into his thick hair, pulling him nearer as his lips part mine. His tongue slips against mine until we can no longer keep our patient pace.

He kisses me like he's giving me his soul to keep. All this time, I've searched for the hybrid that was missing. I didn't realize until now that I, too, was missing. I feel alive with his hands on me, my flesh tingling, a relentless feeling coming to life within me.

A feather light touch moves down my neck, his fingertips trailing along my hot skin before pulling my hip firmly into him. I moan into his mouth at the friction. My back bows of its own accord, trying to eliminate any lingering space between myself and him. His lips leave mine, kissing down my jaw and nipping at my neck. My chest heaves with each breath and the electric current tugs at my core until I can't take it anymore. I grind my hips into his for relief. A low groan escapes his lips into the hook of my neck, the vibrations humming through my chest.

A long and uneven breath leaves me just before his mouth pushes hard against mine again. His teeth rake across my bottom lip in both pain and pleasure before his tongue slips into my mouth and slides against mine. A sweet but salty taste fills my senses.

The feeling of his lips against mine and his hard body grinding into me is stirring a feeling that's restless in my core. It's demanding and threatens to take over entirely. My body works against his to achieve what seems to be the same goal. His hand roams farther across my hip pulling me impossibly closer to him, drifting lower and lower until he stops suddenly, his fingers lingering at the underside of my thigh.

The air leaves my lungs in a heap as he pulls away, my fingers still clutching his neck to me. His chest heaves into mine with each breath he takes. *Why is he stopping?* His heavy gaze never leaves mine. His hair sticks up wildly from where I pulled at it earlier. He licks his lips slowly. I'm reminded of what he tastes like and my body thrums to close the distance again.

"I'm... sorry," he says with a groan. "But I think I should go, before your prince and his, uh," he looks out into the forest, breaking our stare for the first time, "friend finds us."

He's smirking again but I don't know why. *My prince and his friend*? I lean up into his chest, my hands drifting down to his smooth shoulders, refusing to let him go. My heart flutters at our nearness again. My eyes search in the darkness to see what he sees. It takes me a moment to actually focus on something other than his body against mine. Once my eyes adjust it takes no time at all.

There, against a tree, maybe ten yards away is Kaino and Shane. They're holding each other closely—their bodies difficult to make out in the dark.

"Oh."

Not too difficult... Kaino has the warrior pushed against the tree and they're clutching each other, the commander's lips slipping down the warrior's neck in a worshiping way. *Kissing.* Kaino is kissing him. He's *kissing* another guy. I guess our friendship makes sense now. Kaino doesn't dislike me, he just is the furthest thing from interested.

Asher presses his head into my shoulder and laughs at my surprise.

"You knew Kaino was seeing Shane?" I ask, trying to tear my gaze away from the couple making out in the woods, a shadow of groping hands and tongues.

Asher runs his fingers lightly up my spine, lifting his head, his shining eyes search my face. His touch sends a shiver over my body, pulling my attention back to him.

He's smirking down at me, kneeling between my legs. His other hand pushes my messy mass of curls behind my ear and he has the strangest look in his steely gaze.

"I've made it a point to know things about the mystics here. They're good. Mostly. Kaino is good." His fingers trail my face until his palm settles against my neck. "I'm never going to let anything happen to you again, Fallon." His whisper is slow and promising as he pulls me into his body. His strong arms wrap around me in a hug, the epitome of safety. My eyes close as I listen to the steady beat of his heart.

"Good night," he says in a quiet breath before pressing his lips to my temple and unwrapping himself from me. I watch as he climbs down from my pallet in silence.

It's cold without him near. My lips and body tingle, a shadowing memory of him hums through my veins. After a few minutes, leaves crack under foot below my pallet and I throw myself down as if I've been asleep for hours—instead of where I always want to be.

FOURTEEN
WHY DID I SAY THAT

My training has ceased since Asher's arrival. Declan doesn't mention it, but I make a point of shadowing him as I had before. Hoping to keep my place as understudy, hoping to keep our friendship...

It's late, and I want nothing more than to go to bed, but as an understudy, I have to attend the days meeting before retiring to my bed, where I will surely toss and turn for another night.

Luca and I enter the tent, we're nearly the first to arrive... almost.

A werewolf steps closer to Gabriel, eliminating any space between them. His face is a mass of smooth angry features.

"This isn't your place, pike," the wolf slurs into Gabriel's passive face, pushing his forearm into the hybrids throat, pinning him to a beam supporting the tent.

Asher takes a step toward the two of them, but Gabriel holds his hands up dismissively, his new bionic wrist twisting in the candle light. A smug smirk etches the hybrid's features, the hundreds of freckles across his cheekbones standing out even in the dim lighting.

"I didn't know it was a private affair. Did your lord personally invite you, as he did us?" Gabriel asks, his head tilting slightly at the werewolf whose confidence is faltering as he thinks about what the hybrid just said.

"Release him!" Luca demands, storming toward them, her long steps eating up the dry land.

The wolf bares his teeth, his jaw clenching as he assesses his lord's daughter, her hands held high on the curve of her hip. A moment passes quickly before the wolf lowers his arm from Gabriel's throat, keeping his eyes pinned on the hybrid as he walks away.

Asher's gaze slips over my flesh, igniting a flush to creep up my neck and across my cheeks at the memory of his warm body against mine. A deep, unsteady breath fills my lungs as my eyes dart away from his.

It takes me a few seconds to realize Luca is still assessing Gabriel, she appears to be considering her next moves. She takes a single step toward him before back tracking and quickly taking a seat at the long table.

The wolf that threatened Gabriel sits in the third chair to the left of Lord Raske's seat... Right next to my own seat. Dread sinks into me as I take my seat at his side.

It doesn't take long for the seats to fill and the meeting to begin.

I sit ramrod straight in my chair. The wood bites into my spine but I ignore it. Keeping my eyes focused on Raske while also not retaining a word he says.

Declan sits to my right, I'm by his side as I have been for all of the militia meetings. Kaino sits across from Declan, to the right of Raske. The three of them are speaking in great detail about something that I can't seem to keep my mind on.

I wanted desperately to be here. To be a part of the militia to find Asher.

Wish granted.

Now he sits across from me, at Kaino's side. Throwing knowing glances at me every time I so much as breathe loudly.

And he's so distracting. I get it, you're in unbelievably perfect shape, your body is artwork poured down from the heavens. Does his shirt have to be so tight, though? Does he have to smirk at me every time our eyes meet?

"Fallon?" Declan stares at me unblinking.

I shift my eyes around the full table. Luca sits at the end, eyebrows raised, a faint smirk on her lips. I take a deep breath to release the pressure I now feel building within me from all the eyes that are now solely focused on me.

My eyes wander, pleadingly for someone to repeat whatever the hell he just said. Anyone? Luca? She covers her mouth with her hand as a smile breaks quietly over her features.

Thanks.

"He asked if you could join Luca's squad tomorrow to hunt south of here," Asher says, blatantly smiling at me now.

My eyes narrow accusingly at his smug look.

"Of course," I say, turning my full attention back to Raske.

He nods sternly but doesn't comment on my lack of interest. He turns back to Declan, filling in the week's agenda amongst themselves.

Asher is still watching me and I avoid his eyes, busying myself with my pen and paper.

"You can look away already. She clearly has no interest in pikes either," the wolf to my left says.

His words sting, said harshly and quickly, filled with hate and disgust. His name escapes me but his words are all I need to know about him.

Raske barely acknowledges the comment and continues planning with Declan. Kaino's posture straightens but he ignores the comment, as well. Asher studies him for mere moments before adverting his storming eyes, choosing to stare at the table instead of myself. Gabriel stares blankly at the wolf across from him, the wolf who all but spit in his face. He doesn't look away, his unseeing eyes seeing someone clearly for the first time in a long time.

My breathing accelerates as the word builds momentum in my mind.

Pike. Pike. Pike.

"They're hybrids," I blurt out loudly, almost a scream really.

The warrior stiffens at my side. I look up from my white, clean paper. Communication within the room has fallen away and once again all eyes are on me. I raise my head high and stare into the wolf's dark hate-filled eyes.

"Pike is a slur and an ill-educated one at that. They're hybrids. Just like you're not a dog or a mutt," I say looking his wide frame up and down. His werewolf status is apparent in his posture, his confidence, and now his anger.

He shakes in his seat next to me. His body trembles to release his natural form, a rage-filled form. But control is practiced in ten fold in this community. His fists are clenched on the table tops, his knuckles white, his eyes blazing. Briefly, a snarl escapes his quivering lips, his mouth turning snout like for just an instant before he takes deep breaths, reigning the beast back in.

"Obviously, you have no idea what my interests are. Because you don't know me." I stand, my chair sliding unevenly against the dry dirt.

I walk away in silence into the dark night. I let the full moon shine down on me, the beautiful clear light soaking calming thoughts into my messy mind.

I've just made it into the tree line, stepping over a large branch that is barely seen in the darkness, when a hand clutches firmly around my arm.

Fear and anger spark through my nerves, instinctively I grab the dagger at my waist and turn, plunging the blade into the mystic's shoulder. Pain etches the face before me. But it isn't the hate filled wolf from the meeting. Asher's beautiful face is cast in the white streaks of moonlight that filters in through the leaves above.

I cover my mouth with my hand. *I can't believe I just stabbed him.*

"Asher, I'm so s-"

His hands grip both of my arms and he pushes me harshly against a tree. A slight pain stings through my shoulder blades as the bark bites into my flesh. Confusion creeps over my face.

Then his lips press firmly against mine and I settle into him, the tension leaving me in an instant. He kisses me urgently and strongly, all of his strength pushes at the surface to be released as he kisses my lips.

"I can't believe you said that," he murmurs against my lips quickly before kissing me again.

His tongue slips against my own, caressing mine before his teeth rake over my bottom lip. He holds my head with both hands, his fingers pushing into my messy hair before his hands dive down and lift me in one swooping motion. My legs wrap around him as he holds me against the tree. My hands travel up his smooth chest and my fingers collide with something hard. With my lips still on his, my eyes flutter open and I see the hilt of the dagger still sticking out of his shoulder.

He kisses slowly down my neck. His tongue flicks over my pulse and my breath comes in uneven attempts.

"You spoke out in a room of silence," he says, his

breath hot against my neck as he kisses me there over and over again, building a warmth deep within me.

My hand drifts against his blood stained shirt until my fingers curl around the wooden hilt. I rip the blade out of him with a quick turn of my wrist before throwing it to the ground at our feet.

"Fallon," he groans loudly into my neck, his muscles pulled tight beneath my touch from the agony that I just released into him. He bites my neck lightly, a hum of a growl still pulsating over his lips and into me. I shudder a breath as pain flashes into me but it doesn't hurt, it's a different kind of pain. A good pain. My back arches against him as I slowly release the breath I was holding.

He flicks his tongue over the shallow puncture wound, healing the wound instantly and I feel my body hum to life. An energy and warmth spread through my heart and settles under the flesh beneath his mouth.

"Fallon, I," he says kissing back up my jaw as I grind my hip against his.

I pull his hair roughly until we are face to face again and his lips are against mine, his tongue tinged with a faint copper-like taste. His hips align with mine perfectly and I can feel him against every inch of my body, his fingers digging into my thighs as he holds me to him.

"Fallon, I love you," he says in a harsh whisper—more words that my mind isn't grasping at the moment.

But he stops kissing me abruptly, pulling my attention back to his words. Replaying them in my mind until the meaning surfaces there.

His mouth is parted and his eyes are wide as he looks down at me. His lips are swollen from kissing me and a trickle of blood clings to his bottom lip. He licks it away as he slowly releases his hold on me. My feet touch the ground, I'm grounded again. I can think again.

My heart pounds hard against my ribs.

Did he really just tell me he loved me?

"Why did I say that to you?" He asks, mirroring my own confusion.

What he just said stings against my chest but I don't know why. We're friends and his thoughts are just as chaotic as mine are.

"Did you mean it?" I ask in a quiet and nervous voice.

He licks his lips again and takes a step back from me, my hands fall away from him and hang numbly at my side. He swallows hard, his Adam's apple bobbing.

Then he nods heavily before taking another step back as he looks at the dry leaves at our feet.

"Yeah, I did," he says and looks back at me, his wide and terrified eyes searching mine.

For the first time, I see fear there. Mixed in with the severe white and brilliant silver, there's fear. My heart both melts and shatters all at once and I'm not able to form thoughts or words.

He loves me?

"I have to go," he says abruptly.

"Asher, wait."

I reach out to him, my fingers slipping through the

cool air, but he's gone before the words even leave my lips. Quietness and confusion are all that surrounds me.

"So wait, wait, wait," Luca says, repeating herself for probably the third time now as I recall one of the most embarrassing moments of my life to her.

Again.

"So just to be clear, the super sexy hybrid, throws you against a tree, kisses you – which, by the way, I'm going to need a bit more detail on – bites you, confesses his love for you and you do what?"

"Nothing, I-"

"Nothing, right. Yeah, good choice." Her nose wrinkles as she nods enthusiastically at me.

She takes a large bite of a red apple. The crisp crunching sound lingers in the air around us. We sit at a dinner table, just the two of us. People mill around us laughing and eating and enjoying the cool evening weather.

Asher didn't visit me last night. I slept alone in a fit of nightmares that attacked my mind, waking long before the sun rose in an attempt to escape them.

"Can we talk about something else now?" I ask in a defensive tone, raising my eyebrows and my voice all at once.

"I don't know, I don't think anything else will be as

entertaining as this," she says, dripping sarcasm into every word.

She's right, my humiliation and his anguish won't fade anytime soon.

Why did I freeze up? Why didn't I say anything? *Anything*. Because anything would have been better than saying nothing to him.

God, his face. I never want to see his face like that ever again. Because of me.

I push my plate away from me, folding my arms on the wooden table, wishing I could throw my head down and pout like a child. But I can't, and Luca won't let me.

"But, just so we're clear, after he said I love you—"

I lean my head back, staring up at the dark, starry sky and wishing they would fade away into the sun, and that it, too, would crawl back over the sky and I could travel back to last night. If I could have just said how I felt.

If I only knew how I felt.

FIFTEEN
A TOUCHY BREED

AMID ALL OF my jumbled thoughts and awful bad timing, Raske has decided to go ahead with his plan to bring peace with a mortal and mystic union.

"The four of you will go to the camp and mingle with your people, Fallon. You still have friends there, yes?" Lord Raske asks as he addresses Luca, Kaino, Declan and myself.

I nod, thinking of all the people my mother helped at the camp over the years. She was a doctor. The local clinic was only allowed to see the dying. The sick had to fend for themselves and often sought out my mother's help.

My stomach turns just thinking about how many of them have died without a physician.

"Good, walk around with Kaino and Luca, make yourselves seen. Explain. Explain our community.

Explain where you've been and how free and wonderful it all is—how happy you are."

How happy I am. My thoughts drift to Asher and his confession as well as my twisting and disorganized feelings. I nod anyway, agreeing to my supposed happiness. From the corner of my eye, I see Gabriel followed by Asher walk into the tent. They stand back, talking quietly among themselves as we finish up our meeting.

"Declan, you're to stay unseen. You're an outstanding warrior but your presence in the human community just won't work in our favor."

"Of course," the hybrid says as he drums his fingers absently against the wooden table.

Raske turns toward his son, Kaino. He and Shane listen closely for what their lord has to say, but his words never leave his mouth.

"I'd like to go as well," Asher says as he strides up to the end of the table, a pleasant look filling his features. My shoulders tense from the sound of his voice, as if he might tell me he loves me all over again and then disappear the moment he says it. "The community knows Fallon was *taken* by a hybrid. Let her explain herself, explain the mystics in the naturally good light we always seem to be in." He smirks but no one else shares his humor, aside from Gabriel who clasps his friend's shoulder, the two of them passing a sarcastic look between themselves.

Kaino and Luca look to their father immediately who simply stares at the hybrid as if he's suggested we all start doing some quiet book clubs at night instead of celebrations.

"Unfortunately, that doesn't sound like a good idea, Asher. The humans are a touchy breed, their emotions run higher than ours."

My head turns slowly toward the mystic seated at the head of the table, my narrowed eyes focusing only on him.

"A touchy breed?" I repeat carefully, in an attempt to find a less disparaging meaning.

I wonder if he'd still think we were pathetically emotional if he knew how much his son cared for the werewolf seated next to him. If he knew his daughter hasn't stopped talking about a redheaded hybrid since he blindly walked into this community. If he knew that I can't even begin to explain my emotions let alone feel them.

"The human society has just been raised that way, Fallon. I'm not belittling your race." His warm eyes smile down at me and I force myself not reply.

"As I was saying, the plan has been made. I appreciate your interest but now is not a good time to introduce a hybrid into a human society."

My fists clench at my sides, beneath the table my hands are little wads of fury.

"Asher's going. The humans will wrap their tiny minds around my friendship with the hybrid. They'll understand that genetics don't decide if someone is good or bad. They'll see the good in Asher, just like I do."

The room couldn't be quieter if we were all dead. Luca's dark brows are raised so high I wonder if she wishes we were.

I shouldn't have said all that.

My heart pounds as I look to Asher at the opposite end of the table. The corner of his lips pull up into a hesitant but arrogant smile.

"Then it's settled." Asher raises his palms up as if everything is crystal clear now. "The humans will love me as much as your princess does," he says with a wink, not allowing any room for protest as he strides from the tent.

It surprises me how close the secret community of mystics is to my camp. Weeks passed when I traveled from the camp to Asher's grandparents' house. The mystics are faster than humans. All it took was a quiet statement from Kaino about how much faster it would be if we all ran to the camp.

"I could always carry you," Declan says to me with a playful smile that gains him glares from everyone in the group.

"Not a chance," Asher says, stepping between Declan and I as I fasten my backpack around my stomach, my fingers fumble, the clasps falling from my hands when his hard body presses against my side.

"Kaino's right, though, we'd make better time if

you let me help you," Asher says in a whisper as he takes the clasps from my hands, his fingers brushing against my bare stomach. My shirt is short and reveals soft flesh to him, making my breath catch with every movement of his hands. He buckles my pack around my midsection but his hands slip over my sides, almost holding me against him, but not quite. My palms land on his forearms, but I don't dare move another inch.

We're on the outskirts of the community, at the edge of the forest. No one can see us here, other than the three others traveling with us.

"Let me help you," he says in a gravelly whisper, his mouth pressed against my ear, sending shivers across my skin with every hot breath he takes.

I clear my throat and nod, my heart beating wildly in my chest as my mind fills with inappropriate thoughts. My eyes dart around to the others. Luca's eyes are wide as she watches us intently with a smile.

Declan starts off without a word, running into the forest in a blur of blonde movement. Asher smirks and I push his shoulder lightly as I roll my eyes. He bites back his amusement as he lifts me in his arms, our eyes meeting once I'm held safely against his strong chest. All humor is gone. His eyes dip to my lips for only a second before he begins running.

I yelp as my hands cling around his neck. My stomach drops with a sense of diving as we run at a speed that I can't even imagine. I try to focus on the person running next to us but my stomach twists uncomfortably as my eyes strain to see clearly.

I bury my face in his chest, breathing in his warm scent as I wait for the ride to be over. Praying I won't be sick before we get there.

It takes two long days for us to make it to the camp. I only puked once. It's something I take pride in admitting. The others don't consider it an achievement like I do...

"Okay, Declan you know the drill. Stay hidden," Asher tells him with a smirk.

"Why would I hide when you're going to be walking around in plain sight?"

"I'm a friend of a friend. We don't want to send in every hybrid the Wanderers have, it'll look like a revenge ambush for our fallen ancestors," Asher says, dripping sarcasm into every word. He bumps his shoulder casually against Declan's as he passes.

A long sigh passes my lips as I trade a glance with Luca who shares my annoyance.

"*Both of you* will be in hiding," I tell them, stopping Asher in his arrogant tracks. He pauses at my side and slowly nods, his now shaggy dark hair brushing against his ears with the movement. "Stay here in the tree line, don't draw attention to yourselves. I'll gather a crowd later tonight after the patrols have left the village."

The village guards don't linger within the camp after curfew. They'll survey the homes and keep the wealthier people safe and monitored but they can't be spared to keep our camp under watch during the night.

Asher reaches out to me, his warm fingers slipping against mine. "I'll do whatever you ask, Fallon. Just say the word and I'll do it."

My heart flutters and I have to look away from him as his words from the other night trail through my thoughts.

"So we're ready?" Kaino asks as he takes a step toward the camp that is bustling with work in the midday sun that burns down on us.

"Not you. Just Luca," I say, moving closer to my friend.

Kaino's dark brows lower, shading his amber eyes.

"Luca isn't brooding with emotion. The people will like her." The people are also less likely to guess that she's a wolf...

The three mystics that I have fully pushed away are now staring down at me. I've never been in charge before and for a second I'm flooded with authority. A feeling of power almost and the idea of using it against them crosses my mind for an instant before my passive mood returns.

"I'll meet you back here at nightfall."

I remove the belt at my waist, the Crimson Sword swaying in the wind as I hand it to Asher. He stares down at it for a few moments, the sword that was once his but is now mine. I know it'll only cause more questions and that I should leave it behind, but I feel too light without it resting protectively at my side.

Luca and I walk out into the opening, a few men close to the edge of the woods stop and stare at me, pointing and whispering with shifting eyes as I walk toward the center of the camp.

It takes everything I have not to look back for Asher.

The camp's cook, Mrs. Hollis, watches me the entire time that Luca and I eat the sliced apples and the half of a ham sandwich that she was able to spare us. The woman's mouth hasn't closed since I walked through her kitchen door. She holds her hands tightly together, the knuckles turning white as she brushes her fingers back and forth, worrying the thin lines and sun spots that grace her hands.

"Where did he take you, the monster? Everyone's heard, all the surrounding villages, we searched for months..."

The breath catches in my lungs at the use of the word monster. I take a small sip of warm water as I think about her question.

I look over my shoulder, only the kitchen staff and about a dozen intrigued people from outside have wandered into the small room. No guards are in sight. I look to Luca hesitantly, the questioning eyes of the room follow her movements as she weaves around bodies until she's standing at the door, the sun blazing against her smooth caramel skin.

Once Luca is standing watch, I lean over the table prepared to tell Hollis in a hushed tone what happened.

Then I think better of it. My story can't be told in a quiet voice, the voice I used to own, the unsure girl that required her mother's guidance. My mother isn't here anymore, it's just me.

"He isn't a monster." I stand and turn, taking in the dozens of dirty faces that stare back at me. My stomach dips from their attention but I swallow the nervousness down and continue saying what I know has to be said. "The hybrid-vampires are more human than vampire. They've been painted as the villain of our world. They're not. The people oppressing us are."

My voice raises in a commanding and confident tone that I didn't know I possessed. Whispers begin circulating the room as I continue speaking. "The mystics are good and kind. Just like you and me they have their flaws." I pause, realizing how often they celebrate with heavy doses of alcohol and promiscuous behavior, then I shake it off and focus on the people around me. "The mystics are free. They reside in a community just like ours, except the government doesn't interfere with their lives. They're free to unite with whoever they like, they're free to live how they like, with jobs that they enjoy and with as many children as they deem fit for their family."

The women of the room have fallen silent, no more speculating whispers grace their lips. They stare with pain-stricken eyes as they listen to me speak of freedoms they've never experienced.

"We could have that, too. The mystics want us to have that. They want to help us."

"How?" Mrs. Hollis asks, her hands now fisting a dirty towel.

I think about what Raske wants me to sacrifice for all these mystics to have the lives they deserve. Deep down I know I won't, I won't live a life of complacency. I've lived that life for years and it isn't meant for anyone.

"By being informed. By spreading the word. Our government hides the mystic's freedom from us. They abuse us as well as them. Neither of us should be hiding from the other. Information is something we don't have, that's why the hybrids have been misconstrued for generations. Because information comes solely from the group of people that is meant to help us. They aren't helping us. They're controlling us. We need to help ourselves."

A few dazed looking individuals nod back at me and a few remain impassive to my words.

"I'd like you to meet the person that saved me from my life here." Ky's face flashes through my mind as well as Asher's. As well as my mother's... "Meet a mystic just like Luca." The room shifts as a single unit, all bodies turning to stare at the beautiful werewolf, seeing her for what she really is for the first time.

She smiles at them, a look of kindness touching the curve of her lips.

"With the help of many, Luca saved me. Tonight, I ask you all to tell those that you trust, that you care about, that a change can happen in their lives. If they're strong enough to allow it."

I glance to Mrs. Hollis, the woman that shows compassion and strength with her every breath. "I'll arrange a meeting place with Mrs. Hollis. She'll only reveal the location if the person asking is trustworthy of the information." Sweat begins to appear at the woman's brow and she wipes it hastily away as her darting eyes meet mine.

I lean over the hardwood counter now, resting my hand on hers. "Say you'll help us. Say you'll help them as well as yourself," I whisper.

She swallows and adverts her eyes toward the flour-dusted floor. "When I was your age, I wanted kids. Loads of them." Her lip quivers as she takes a big breath, her chest heaving wide with the movement. "I was told I wasn't qualified but my cooking skills were above average. They assigned me to cook for the local school instead." My hand tightens on hers, my chest growing heavier with every word she confesses.

Her breath catches but she continues. "I ran away. I just couldn't let someone else live my life. They found me though and brought me back to the work camp. Sentenced me to live my life here alone, without my unity partner or family or any children. And I've done it. For fifty-six years, I've done nothing but live the life I was told I was qualified to have. We're done with that lifestyle."

She releases my hand and looks to the overflowing

and stifling room full of people. “For those of you that are tired of not having a say in your life, come to me and I will tell you the time and the place for a change.” Her voice booms over the heads of the listening audience. “A change that will promise your children a better life. A life of freedom!”

Anxious smiles greet the cook that everyone knows and respects. My heart leaps at the sight of the responsive community. I whisper a location and hour to the beaming woman and then as quickly as possible, Luca and I scurry back to the woods. Like two mice plotting a secret revolution...

SIXTEEN
HOSTILITY

ASHER SLIPS his fingers through mine, his palm squeezing a jolt of reassurance through me. The five of us stand in the camp's shed. Half a dozen tractors are lined against one wall, outdated and twisted metal shine against the dim lighting in the room. It's as much light as we're willing to risk at this hour of the night.

Kaino stands with his arms folded across his wide chest, a look of impatience filling the commander's stern face.

Luca brushes her arm against his. "Relax your posture. These people have never met a mystic before, they don't want to walk in here and come face to face with a scowling wolf. Smile a little." She nods to her brother.

He thinks for a moment and then uncrosses his arms, she gives him another reassuring nod. Slowly the most conflicting and tense smile fills his face. A smile that makes my stomach drop. A smile that appears false and a little sadistic.

"Don't smile," she says in a rush. "Just, stand toward the back and maybe they won't notice you too much."

Declan smirks and joins me at the center of the room. "You sure this is a good idea? What if they decide to just burn this shack down instead? Get rid of the few mystics that are creeping into their territory."

I turn to him, the shadows hiding his feelings from me. He stuffs his hands into his pockets as he waits for my response. He wants to leave. He doesn't trust these people. Maybe he's afraid they'll reject him. All Declan's ever felt is rejection, he's used to it, he anticipates it. My emotions cloud my chest as I look at him.

"They won't," I tell him. "They're trusting us. We have to trust them, too." I touch his arm and he looks at me, his silver eyes catching the light and holding it in his gaze. He stares at me for a long curious moment before nodding slowly and walking away, back into the shadows.

Footsteps echo through the high rafters—hundreds of footsteps—so many my heart begins to race faster with the sound of each new person walking into the room. Asher squeezes my hands once more before stepping away from me and joining the other three mystics behind me.

Mrs. Hollis stands at the front of the overflowing crowd. They're a mass of black clothing, dignified clothing assigned by the government to keep them cool in the ever rising heat. I glance back at the shirtless men and the cropped shirt that Luca wears that matches my own.

I cross my arms nervously over my stomach, hiding the exposed skin there, feeling more different than these people I grew up with than ever before. I can feel myself beginning to sink to my own self-doubt.

What if we're too different? What if they don't want to work side by side with the mystics? What if they really do just want to burn this place to the ground?

A palm brushes my elbow, I turn, almost expecting Asher but I'm met with the warm eyes of a wolf. Luca smiles at me as she subtly shifts our stance toward the crowd again.

"Thank you all for joining us tonight," she says in a smooth and confident tone. Her capturing voice and assured movements reminding me of her father in this moment. "Fallon appreciates your support and we'll start by hearing her journey. A journey that many of you, in a strange way, might find you relate to."

I stare out at the watchful eyes of the audience that I asked to come here. And I can't think of a single word to say.

Why didn't I write something down? I can physically feel the labor my lungs are putting into guiding air through my chest. Heat begins to flame my face, creeping slowly up my neck and cheeks.

I swallow as I rack my mind for what to say.

"My-" A pause fills my mind as I begin speaking without thought. "My mother was just like you. Just like all of you. She obeyed when she wanted nothing more than to run away. She wasted her life away in the confines of this camp. She watched the one man she loved from a distance, never actually feeling love the way you should." I glance back at Asher as my nerves wash away.

"For those of you who don't know, Charlotte died last year." My voice catches, still echoing around us, and I realize it's the first time I've admitted that she's dead... "She died trying to save me from the life she led. A life that isn't really a life at all. Is it really living if you're emotions are scheduled by the government? Love and family and employment are all dictated to us like animals. We're not animals. The mystics behind me are not animals. We're the same, them and us."

I scan the crowd for an instant. "Except they're free. Hidden but free."

Whispers crawl through the room. Shifting eyes try to decide if I'm lying or not.

"I was raised by mortals, two of the nicest people you'll ever meet," Asher says as he walks to my side. "My mother was human. I'm half human. My friends," He hesitates, the word friend seeming odd in his tone. "they're half human. They're from a society that your government created. A nice little community where people live as they please without magic and without shifting. Kaino is a strong warrior but he hasn't turned into his natural wolf form since he was a child. Because that was the condition of the agreement between the mortals and the mystics. They aren't raging beasts. They can control it. Just like humans can control their temper."

"Until they can't and someone dies!" an unseen voice shouts. The man's anger and hatred carries through the room and gains nods and glares from the others.

Asher shifts on his feet, his arms crossing for an instant. "I could say the same for you. Anyone can lose their temper, man or mystic. The government is breeding hostility among us all."

"If you joined with us, if you let us help you," I tell them, "your lives can only improve. You're worried about death but your people are dying every day. They're being imprisoned for petty, ruthless reasons. Your loved ones, your friends, are not safe here."

I'm met with silence and blinking eyes as my heart begins quivering in my chest.

They don't want our help...

Mrs. Hollis steps forward, the community watches the large and captivating woman's every step. "When do we leave?" Her question hangs in the air like the stifling black sweater that hangs from her shoulders.

My lungs shake as I take in a breath, assurance bubbling within my chest as I speak, "Soon. Really soon."

Our journey home feels different. I should be bursting with hope but instead, tension fills my body. Declan keeps catching my eye as we walk into the forest, just on the outskirts of the camp. His silver eyes reflect the moon as they shift through the dense shadows.

"Did you hear that?" he asks, stopping abruptly in his tracks, his head tilting as he listens to the silence.

Nothing is heard, not even the wildlife dares make a move with the mystics that surround me.

"I don't hear anything," Kaino says.

"Me either," whispers Luca, her shoulders stiff as she scans the area.

In a flash of movement, Asher is at my side, his hand gripping the sword at his hip.

"We should check it out just in case," Declan tells us.

Asher nods, his jaw strung tight as he follows the other hybrid into the clearing. Kaino and Luca move with hushed steps, their tawny eyes judging every angle of our surroundings.

"What do you think it could be?" Luca asks.

"We overheard a few men saying how the compound here closed down last year. The building is just used as a holding space for found mystics until they can be shipped elsewhere. Hundreds of pik—hybrids and a few veil were shipped to the Capitol for further detention and study." Kaino pauses as he turns on the heel of his boot, surveying the quiet shadows more closely. "It's possible that some escaped during the transfer. That's when I would have made my move."

A shiver claws over my skin as my memory flashes with images of the bloody talons of the veil. I shudder, my arms wrapping around myself. That's not possible. None of those things have ever escaped. A hybrid had never escaped until Asher.

I try to find reassurance in the thought but it's no use. My heart pounds louder with every second that passes without Asher and Declan's return.

A growl echoes through the darkness, rustling up birds and fearful animals through the woods. A jostling rustling sound comes from where Asher and Declan disappeared.

"Something's wrong," Luca says.

I take a step toward the camp but Kaino's thick arm wraps around me in an instant.

"Don't move," he whispers.

"You're just going to let him get ripped to shreds?" I ask, my voice quivering on a scream.

"It's not veil, Fallon," Luca tells me, as she hunches down in the shadows of the forest. "It's humans."

The three of us are motionless as her words settle into my mind, a tightness clutching at my chest.

Declan runs toward us, stopping just a foot from me. "I tried to stop them, but they took him." His brow creases. "I'm so sorry, Fallon."

I'm thrashing in Kaino's arms before Declan can even finish speaking. The wolf releases me and I stumble, my feet slipping against the dry leaves as I race to the clearing. Tree limbs tear at my skin but the pain doesn't register. I run out into the opening just as tail lights turn out of sight.

Heading toward the compound.

SEVENTEEN
IN THE DEAD OF NIGHT

THE WARM AIR burns my lungs as I trail after the truck that hauled him away. Panic grips my chest, making the simple task of breathing even harder. I force my feet to move faster, faster to the one place I never want to see for the rest of my life.

It's then that I know.

I love him.

The thought knocks me off balance and the ground greets me as my feet stumble in their pace. The fabric of my dark jeans rips at the knee, scuffing the hard earth against my flesh. My palms brace me above the dry dirt.

Luca touches my shoulder lightly, her warm palm slipping over my sweaty skin. "You need to think about what you're doing. You're putting us all in danger by not thinking this through," she says in a calm voice. Her hand drifts up and down my spine, comforting me as I fall apart.

"They took him... Again," I say in a gasp.

"I know. We'll get him back."

Her hand drifts to my upper arm and she lifts me from my defeated slump.

I take another shaking breath and try my best to listen to her reasoning. We need to think this through. We can get him back. We will. We have to.

"How many of them were there?" I ask, turning toward Declan.

He stands at Kaino's side, the two commanders waiting for my instruction.

"One."

My back stiffens as anger fuels my body. "One?" I repeat in an exasperated tone. "How did one human overpower the two of you?" I'm striding toward him, adrenaline and irrationality controlling my heavy steps.

"He shot off a dart into Asher's shoulder. I...I didn't stick around to wait for the dart with my name on it."

Kaino remains standing with perfect posture as he turns his head slowly toward the hybrid at his side. "You left him there? You left a fellow warrior behind?"

"He isn't a warrior," Declan replies, his eyes narrowing to thin slits. "I could have gotten us all captured if I had stuck around."

My fists clench at my side but I don't have time to discuss this right now.

I trail down the dirt path, the deep divots and rough rocks disrupting my determined pace. Luca, Kaino, and Declan follow close behind. The four of us cling to the shadows, which isn't hard to do in the dead of night.

The towering brick walls of the compound come into view and a bit of respite seeps through me. The white truck that took him away is parked outside. A single guard stands watch at the entrance of the building.

We assess the area from a few yards away, crouched behind a large and pungent smelling garbage bin. It reeks of rotting food, and... carcasses. My stomach churns, threatening to throw up the smell that's strangling my lungs.

"Kaino, do you think you can manage the guard?" Luca asks, leaning around the dumpster for a closer look.

The warrior nods, his face stern as he begins to stand.

"I'll do it," Declan says, taking a single step before my hand wraps tightly around his wrist.

"No, Kaino will manage," I tell him through gritted teeth, not chancing a glance at the hybrid I'm now beginning to doubt.

Kaino stalks through the night, his boots picking up pace the closer and closer he strides toward the man. In a flash, he appears before the guard. His large hands covering the man's mouth and majority of his face as muffled screams are heard.

The two of them stand like that for several moments, the sounds becoming more and more faint with each passing second until the man's body loses strength. He slumps forward and Kaino finally releases him. He drops to the ground, his legs crumpled awkwardly beneath him.

The three of us join the commander. "He won't be out long," Kaino tells us, his deep eyes expressionless as he looks at me.

A small part of me warms, seeing him as a real friend for the very first time. Kaino could have easily killed that man. It would have been easier, safer even. But he didn't.

Drawing my sword, I grip the cold metal handle and open the door. The lobby is vacant and dark, void of the staff that once filled this morbid facility. I glance toward the work chamber that the hybrids once filled. Through the window, an empty and messy room is seen as if the hybrids were jerked from this place without notice.

I can't help but wonder if too much damage was done. Shaw released countless veil into the world just to capture Asher. Too many lives were lost, his own life was lost. The government had to do clean up and they couldn't risk someone else jeopardizing their precious pikes the way Shaw did.

Or perhaps they just wanted to use them first hand...

With cautious steps, I move farther into the compound, my body hugging the wall of the hallway as we walk to where the tests were done. I'm not familiar with the layout of the compound. When my mother worked here, I chose to stay in the lobby, but I know the awful things that must have happened here. My nerves can almost sense the wrongness of this place. The years of abuse that stains the walls, I can physically feel it crawling over my skin.

Looking around the corner, I spot a single guard sitting outside a steel door. His head is tipped back, his eyes closed as his chest rises and falls steadily.

Luca spots the guard as well, stepping carefully past me, her silent steps drifting over the dirty tile floor. She stands before the man and slowly leans toward him, her aggressively playful eyes watching him closely, her nostrils flaring, fanning her breath over his face.

It only takes a moment for the man to realize something is off. His even breaths halt, his body no longer filled with relaxation. Tension fills his shoulders as his eyes slowly open, blinking up at the warrior before him. His arms jerk, the chair scraping against the floor with the sudden movement. A smile consumes her features, her eyes lighting up like he's the most amazing man she's ever seen.

Her lips begin to quiver, her jaw shaking almost violently as she pins him with a glowing stare. She bares her teeth just as her jaw cracks, the snout of a wolf aggressively snarling where her full lips once were. The man flinches from her, his eyes scrunching tightly closed, pressing himself against the chair to create space between him and the mystic. A growl passes over Luca's grimacing lips, a bark snaps from her mouth before she shakes her head, her face and features returning to the beautiful woman once again.

In a single breath, she says a word that throws him into frantic motion. "Run."

He pushes past her, flailing against the smooth tile as he struggles with the exit door, finally pushing it open and rushing into the night.

Luca grips her stomach as her echoing laugh fills the hall, her shoulders shaking as she breathes out a happy sigh. "Did you see the look on his face?" She wipes a tear from her eye as she walks back to us.

"Are you done?" Kaino asks, quirking a brow at his sister's antics.

She licks her lips, smoothing the enormous smile from her face and nods.

I walk past her. "Is anyone else here?" I ask.

Kaino turns his head listening down the hall, possibly even the entire building. "No one else."

Straightening my shoulders, I stand back from the thick metal door. "Open it," I command, staring unflinchingly at Declan.

For a quiet moment, his gaze locks with mine, considering me—the only real friend he has—before he slowly moves passed Kaino. He holds the slim handle in his palm, he turns it but it doesn't fully twist. His fist tightens and a snapping sound fills the air as the handle rotates full circle. Leaning his shoulder in, he pushes the door with force until it finally swings open.

My heart leaps and I rush by him. I nearly trip on Asher as I burst into the room. Just inside the room, he lies on his side on the dusty floor. His limbs strewn out at his sides. I kneel at his side but his breathtaking eyes don't open to me. My hand clutches his, my fingers darting out, reaching for his pulse at his wrist. It beats wildly beneath my fingertips, just like he said it did. It beats for me.

EIGHTEEN
HYSTERIA

WE RETURN to the Wanderers by the following night but it isn't at all the community we left behind. The tree that should welcome us is split down the center. The words Wanderers Welcome isn't at all a comforting sight. It's encompassing and ancient limbs lay haphazardly against the ground, Half of it leans, putting effort into remaining in place, while the other half drapes across the forest.

Kaino and Declan race into the magic shielded community, Luca and I trailing behind them as she heaves Asher across her shoulders, readjusting the weight of the hybrid as she jogs.

The community fumes with black smoke, two fae use their power to diminish the leaping flames that are threatening to burn the trees and the community from existence. Water flows from their palms, putting out minimal flames as more and more seem to grow.

I cough into my arm, squinting my eyes against the

tendrils of smoke. I know what's happened before we even make it to the tent.

"They knew they couldn't see us to fight us, they can't enter here if they aren't welcome, so they did what mortals always do," Raske tells his son. The lord's solemn eyes study the ground. "They bombed us in the middle of the night, racing off into the sky, refusing to fight for what they believe in."

Luca stands with Asher still strung over her strong shoulders, but her eyes show weakness and fear. "How many lives were lost?"

"We heard them coming. The dirt bags don't understand it's a little hard to surprise a wolf," a lazy smile touches his lips for just an instant. "We evacuated the land in mere seconds. Everyone's safe."

I close my eyes and take a deep breath. No one else has died. Everyone's fine.

For now.

Everyone works through the night, restoring the community to the pristine condition by sunrise. The wreckage of the attack barely left a shadow on these unbreakable people. Even the huts are right back in place. The materialistic items may be gone but everything else appears... untouched.

The only significant difference is the Welcoming tree. The massive historical tree can never be replaced. I point out a large tree in the area but Kaino didn't even give the elder tree a glance.

As I walk with him, I find him dwelling on a small

tree, a tree so insignificant it might be trampled over by a deer or low flying owl on any given day.

"This one," he says, flicking open a knife as he kneels at the base of the tiny sapling, the branches barely sweeping above his black hair. He studies the trunk, not larger than his forearm, before haphazardly etching the words *Wanderers Welcome* into the smooth bark.

"Kaino, that one might not make it through the year," I tell him in a tired voice, not really caring at this point.

"It'll make it." He finishes his carving, his dark fingers trailing over each letter. "Strength isn't an appearance, Princess. It's a presence, a feeling kept in your core, waiting to be freed." He peeks over his shoulder at me, his depthless eyes meeting mine. "You were once this tree. A year ago, Luca drug home a puny human girl I thought for sure wouldn't make it through the night. Yet, here you stand. Commanding a commander through a human village just to save one hybrid."

As he stands, I try to suppress the smile that's wide across my lips. I look up at him as he avoids my gaze, shifting uncomfortably.

"Stop," he says, looking at the burnt ground instead of my beaming happiness.

"Why?"

"Because."

"Does affection really make you that uncomfortable, Kaino?"

He ignores me, the serious stiffness set in his stern features once again.

The image of Kaino entangled with Shane flashes through my mind and I manage to bite back my smile and teasing. Kaino really is my friend and if he isn't ready to be himself... then I shouldn't press him. I just want him to be happy. Shane makes him happy but he refuses to fully accept that fact. Or perhaps his father would never accept that fact.

Exhaustion tears at my lethargic body as I look up at the sound of approaching footsteps. I pull my sword as Michael walks our way, his eyes darting over the concealed community. He see's nothing but he knows what's here.

In an instant, Kaino starts running toward the representative. Ayden appears at Michael's side just as Kaino leaps through the magic shielding force, shifting from man to wolf in the blink of an eye. His limbs seem to tear open, his skull pulling back for the beast that thrashes to be released.

The commander lands on four paws at Michael's feet, sending the man crawling backward, scuttling through the leaves to find some distance between himself and the snarling black wolf. Kaino's beautiful, so much so, that I stop in my tracks, staring wildly at the beast I always knew was within him.

His fur shines against the morning light, a look of strength and power in his massive form. His always straight spine ends in a swaying, unkempt tail that stops moving as his depthless eyes hold the stare of my father.

Ayden backs carefully away, his hands out in front of him in a gesture of surrender.

I trail after the aggressive animal, running until I, too, exit the shielded community.

"Fallon, tell him to stop!" Michael cries as Kaino takes a prowling step closer.

Why are they here? Just the two of them?

"Kaino, wait," I beckon as his head dips lower, a rippling growl passing over his sharp canines.

"You have a lot of nerve coming here," Lord Raske says as he steps up beside me. "I should kill you myself. I could send your tongue back to your president as a parting gift for all the lies she told us."

"We're not here for war. I wasn't aware of the attack until this morning. Ayden and I came as soon as we could. We don't support the bombing but we can only urge you not to proceed with your plans. Just lie low and this could all blow over. She said it was meant as a message. Just accept the message. Stop trying to change what you have."

My eyes narrow on him, on the sweat that's slipping down the side of his jaw, at the quiver in his weak voice, at the man that's supposed to be my father. Not at all like the father figure that I loved; not anything like Ky.

Ayden pulls at Michael's arm and cautiously helps the man stand, his brass eyes wide as he holds the stare of the deadly wolf before him.

"If the Wanderers are anything, they are resilient, they are unyielding, they are valiant." Raske's eyes are hooded, his brow pressed low over his irate glare. "Do not threaten my people—my family—and expect us to look the other way."

Michael glances at me, my father looking at me for the first time since his president attacked us. Attacked me...

"Your people are my people," he says in a quiet voice, his shoulders falling as he keeps his eyes on mine.

My heart pounds, my lips falling open without a sound, his admission sending a blooming feeling through my chest.

Raske turns his back on my father, sending him a single message as he leaves, "You know nothing of these people."

My father doesn't know me at all. He should have protected me. All my life he should have protected me.

You know nothing of these people.

He's right.

"Have you decided, Fallon?" Raske asks, nothing but kindness and concern fill his deep amber eyes. He looks at me the way a father would look at his daughter. He speaks to me the way a father would console a daughter. And yet, he doesn't acknowledge Luca in the least, and she returns his sentiment.

"No, I have not decided," I say in an even tone as if we're discussing which dessert we might eat after dinner.

How can he even be thinking about this after what just happened? A union won't fix the damage that's been done. The suggestion of a biracial union is what caused this mess. President Docile said they'd return to check on us.

And so they did.

The thought of what they did to this community burns anger and hate through my veins like I've never felt before, setting my fists tight and my mind reeling.

"I don't mean to pressure you. It's just," he pauses, scrunching his brows as he thinks, "with the bombing... There's still a chance to unite the mortals and the mystics. The races once worked together against a greater evil... We could do it again..." He can't seem to find the right words to convey his thoughts. "Everyone's morale is a little down... You don't seem taken with anyone really. I know for a fact you have more than enough offers. I watch males flag you down daily, but you don't give them the time. You have to make friends with the wind if you ever expect to fly."

I want so badly to roll my eyes at his remark but somehow I remain neutral to his ridiculous words.

"I am not unkind. I'm just..."

"Uninterested?" He finishes for me.

I laugh loudly at his remark. Unable to keep the hysterical noise within my tired body.

His brows rise at my brash behavior and it makes me laugh more. The people cleaning up the fallen limbs and debris pause to take notice of my fit of laughter. Asher smiles into his glass, cocking an eyebrow at me over the brim. Kaino continues to talk to the hybrid as if I'm not sitting before them all like a hyena on laughing gas.

"The finest warriors in our community are funny to you? My son is funny to you?" Raske's stern voice rises. He is no longer amused by my inappropriateness.

The reminder of Kaino sneaking around behind his father's back to be with Shane surfaces in my mind and I can't help but laugh some more, touching my palm to my aching stomach as the uncontainable laughter swirls within me.

"You do understand that these mystics have been watching you with bated breath, for you to take an interest in any one of them and you do nothing but laugh in their faces for their efforts. I'm not forcing you, Fallon, but you could at least have the courtesy to take them seriously."

My labored breath halts entirely, the laughter is sucked from my body. All the hysteria leaves me and is replaced with anger. The emotional flow is so quick and my lungs can't catch up. I clench my jaw and raise my raging eyes to meet his.

Asher and Kaino stop speaking, those around us stop speaking. My silence is passing into them and it's as if they can feel my mood that's boiling to the surface, threatening to spill over onto them.

"The courtesy?" I ask loud and annunciating. "You think I owe your people a courtesy?" My eyes are wide, my lips thinning between words, pressing tightly together as my mind swirls in a flow of angry thoughts. "Every man here, and a few women as well, have embarrassingly approached me as if I'm a pet to play with. To take home and entertain their *lord* with."

"Fallon, this is not how we should discuss this. We should talk privately-"

"No, this is something everyone needs to hear," I say, cutting him off, my eyes shifting from him to the large crowd around us. The crowd that's watching me intently. "I am not your entertainment. I am not a chess piece to be played and pushed around the board. I am not an obstacle stopping you from living your lives and I most definitely am not a prize. I won't join someone who sees me as a piece to be played, an obstacle or especially a prize."

My narrowed eyes scan the mass of people before me. The males hold my glare and the females nod their heads in agreement. My loud words are shouted into the silence and are absorbed into their minds, to be understood or to be misconstrued but the words are taken all the same.

Asher does his best to remain impassive but I can see how his eyes are lit up with interest at my angry seminar I'm now holding. Kaino's arms are crossed but he isn't angry, he, too, is intrigued, his naturally tense features smoothing slightly. Luca smiles widely from nearby, all but cheering me on.

"I am not your opponent and I will not bow to a mystic who does not see me as a teammate." Luca nods giving me courage. A strange fear and nervousness presses heavily into my lungs as I realize what I am about to do.

"With that being said," I pause, walking slowly up to Asher, his brilliant silver eyes never leave mine, but search my face for any indication of what I'm about to do so publicly. "Asher Xavier... would you..." My mind searches for the word his grandpa used over a year ago. It's foreign and my tongue struggles to pull it from my memory. I bend one knee, bowing before him like a servant to her master. "Would you marry me?"

I'm breathing hard but I keep a façade of calm in my features as I look up at him. His lips quirk, tilting up into a small smile. The crowd around us hums to life. Words flow quietly from one person to the next, as everyone waits for Asher's reply.

As I wait for his reply.

"If you don't marry her someone else will," Gabriel shouts from behind us making me smile. A flush of red creeps over my face, making me even warmer.

Asher shakes his head, my heart falling a little with each passing second. He drops to his knees before me, a soldier surrendering to his conqueror, lowering himself to my level. Only a foot of space is between us as we kneel in the dirt together.

"I'll ruin your life, baby," he says quietly, touching his fingers lightly to the inside of my palms, not holding them but brushing his fingers against the inside of my hands. His touch is reassuring despite his words.

"I can do that all on my own. That's not what I asked

you." His dimples appear, his perfect smile widening at my words. "I'm asking you to not screw it up any more than it already is," I tell him.

He nods, leaning in and pressing his forehead to mine. I breathe him in, my eyes held wide open, not wanting to miss a word he says.

This is us. Always desperate for the other to catch up. Always patiently waiting for one to realize what the other sees. The world might always press in on us, but he continues to hold the sky up for me to walk this earth safely. I'd let the sky fall down around us if it meant I could be in his arms in the end.

"Well, how can I refuse a proposal like that?" he asks loudly for everyone to hear.

He presses his lips lightly to mine. I take a deep breath as happiness and reassurance wash into me.

Luca shouts and cheers as the crowd around us erupts in applause, making me blush even more as I smile against his lips.

NINETEEN
THE BONDING

THE FOLLOWING day is spent in a whirlwind of energy. Not from me. The most I accomplish is a few yawns, exhausted from just watching Luca scramble around with unity items—*Wedding* items.

In my camp, a unity is completed in document form. Signing, agreeing and moving on with your new lives together.

Apparently, that is not what this is. A unity and a marriage are clearly not the same thing. I'm starting to wonder if a marriage is sleep deprivation, tears and anxiety.

The *most beautiful day of my life* another mystic told me, as she fought the layers of white material in her hands. She's made me nervous with all the tearing and sewing and ripping I've watched her do for the last few hours.

I take another gulp of my drink, letting it burn the

back of my throat as Luca twists and pulls every hair on my head. My head tilts painfully back and forth beneath her strong hands.

"Are you sure all this stuff is needed? Asher already knows what I look like. Changing my hair and clothes for one day isn't going to make him love me any more than he already does."

"It's needed, now sit up straighter or we're going to be here all day," she snaps at me.

My back goes ramrod straight at her sharp words.

Okay. Someone is a little more invested in this event than I am.

"Why white? And why a dress?"

I don't think I've ever worn an elaborate dress like this in my life. The flowing material covers the table in front of us in a heap of tulle and crisp white fabric.

The dirt and dry air are going to destroy that pretty thing.

"Well, miss negativity, years ago, white was a symbol of innocence and virginity."

I spew my drink into my cup and down my chin and neck. I cough as the liquid burns my throat and lungs.

"And why, might I ask, is my *innocence and virginity* anyone's business?" I ask still trying to breathe properly.

She snorts loudly, tugging harshly at my thick long hair.

"It's definitely not anyone's business. But it used to be. It used to be an incredibly important foundation for a marriage."

A pause fills the silence as my mind wanders.

"Do you think it's important to Asher? That I'm not," I pause keeping my eyes down, inspecting the bottom of my empty cup, "that I'm not experienced?" My voice is shaky and quiet. There isn't an ounce of confidence in me at the moment.

"Of course not, Fallon." She stops working for a moment, her hands resting comfortably on my shoulders. "Asher loves you. I promise everyone is just as unsure of themselves at some point in their lives as you are right now. But not everyone has someone who loves them like Asher loves you." Her words are gentle and fill my heavy heart. "You guys have each other. You guys will discover everything together."

"Thanks, Luca," I say in a whisper, tilting my head up to meet her eyes, my lungs breathe easier just thinking about her words.

Luca's an amazing person. Someone I never expected to meet after what I went through. And I don't know if I could have made it through this last year without her.

"Besides, with a body like his, I doubt you'll be able to think about anything once he's naked."

A smirk fills my lips, my eyes slipping closed as heat flames my face.

"You're such a romantic," I say with an eye roll as we burst into laughter.

Music strums gently into the cool breeze, a noise soft and familiar. The salt of the ocean fills the air around me. A long white curtain separates me from everyone else. I can see the shadows of the people seated beyond the curtain. A figure stands alone at the edge of the cliff.

My fingers push nervously at the white fabric of my dress. The thin material flows intricately, sliver-like pieces caress my legs, exposing tan skin against the stark white color. The bodice is tight against my chest making my unsure breaths harder to take. My hair hangs around me in elaborate twists and a few thick braids at the top before cascading down one shoulder in a tangle of thick curls.

Luca applied a black gel to my lashes making them impossibly longer and more defined. She stained my lips a deep red before finally setting her tools down and looking at me. Declaring me ready to be *wed*.

I breathe out slowly, the air running quickly over my lips. I fidget with the thin strip of tulle at my waist but my hand is slapped away at my side. A stinging pain bursts over my knuckles as I glare up at my friend beside me.

"Calm down already, you're making me nervous. I'm not a nervous person, Fallon. It's not a good look for me," Luca says smiling warmly at me.

"What will we do once we're out there?" I ask, my eyes scanning the hundreds of people sitting on the other side of the curtain.

"Well, she'll say a few words, joining the two of you as man and woman. We'll do the ceremonial Bonding then you'll..." She tilts her head back and forth before shrugging.

I glance quickly her way. She ignores my look and stares straight ahead.

"No, I don't know. What? What will we do, Luca?"

She's quiet still. Her lips thinning. She says nothing.

"What?" I ask loudly, almost shrieking.

A few people turn in their seats toward the sound of the frantic human screaming over the beautiful strumming music.

"You'll jump!" she finally yells.

"Jump? We're going to jump?" She nods her head at me in confirmation. "We're going to jump... off the cliff? Into the ocean?"

Again, she nods slowly as fear crashes over me. Memories of how hard it was for me to swim in the still unmoving water of the cave rush back to me.

"Luca, I can't swim. Why didn't you tell me this? Why would cliff jumping be a part of this? Can we just skip it? I can't drown on my unity day! You spent an hour on my hair just so I could drown on my unity day?" I ask manically.

"It's a wedding, Fallon, not a union."

"Whatever," I shriek back at her, stomping my bare foot against the dirt.

My eyes are wide and my breathing is fast but unproductive. The pounding of my heart is so loud I no longer hear the music. *Is the music still playing?*

Through the curtain I see Asher's silhouette walk

toward us, closer to where I stand, having an anxiety attack over something that shouldn't even be an issue on my unity day.

Luca whips the curtain back, exposing her head but nothing else.

"We're fine. Everything is fine. It'll just be another moment. Thank you all for your patience," she says smiling prettily, Asher stops in his tracks, hesitantly. "I said we're fine," she growls at him, baring her teeth menacingly.

His hands fly up in a defensive stance before backing away to stand at the edge of the cliff again.

"I didn't want to make you nervous. Jumping is the closing of the ceremony. It's an old ritual done in our culture for centuries. The couple jumps as an offering to the ocean, and if they are not a true match, a perfect match, the water fae will correct the error and whisk away the untrue heart."

"What? I'm not only jumping into the ocean off of a cliff," I say slowly, "but then I have to hope water fae don't drag me under as I doggie paddle my way back to land? Does Asher know about this, about the... the water fae?"

She nods impatiently, peeking back around the curtain at the audience.

Luca drops the drape back down and spins on her heels to look at me, fury and determination in her eyes.

"Do you love Asher?" she asks loudly.

I do. I haven't said it yet, to anyone, not even him. But I do.

I nod my head slowly, forcing air into my lungs, fighting the tight bodice for air.

"Then trust him. Believe that when you leap, he won't let you fall, and he would never let anyone take you away from him. Because he won't, Fallon."

I take another shaky breath and nod stiffly at her. She's right. Of course, she's right. I'm being dramatic. I'll be fine. It's fine.

"Are you ready?" she asks, her hand already clutching the curtain.

I tilt my head up, smoothing my dress and wiping the sweat from my shaking hands against the nice fabric, forcing my nerves away.

I nod at her again, my head bobs with vigor.

She smirks at me and laces her fingers through mine. Her hand is cool and steady against mine.

The music hums through the air again. It's possible that it never stopped but I really have no idea.

Luca slowly pulls back the curtain and leads me into the crowd of Wanderers. There are hundreds of them. Kaino stands at the front, near the edge of the cliff. Lord Raske smiles broadly at me from the front of the crowd. Gabriel waves his bionic fingers at me, his eyes focused intently on Luca, who smiles shyly at him.

And then I see him.

Standing at the edge of the world, the ocean dark behind

him, the sun surrounds him, sinking low into the water. The sea breeze lifts his dark hair, like a whirl of emotions flowing around him. And his beautiful silver eyes are glistening as he looks at me. His eyebrows rise slightly, his lips parting, his intense eyes drifting over my exposed body.

The nerves that were drowning me just seconds ago are washed away under his gaze. I walk confidently toward him, closer and closer, wanting to ambush him where he stands, among all the people. My bare feet pick up the pace against the dirt and I realize the music is strumming around us.

I look for the source of the perfect melody. My eyes drift over the crowd until I realize, next to Asher, at his right-hand side, is his grandfather.

Jim stands smiling at me, his fingers moving effortlessly against the cords of his guitar. The gray hair that was so disorderly when I first met him, is now neatly combed back from his lined face. Shae stands proudly at his side, the wind ruffling her long silver hair, piled high on her head. They look so out of place against the ocean side but I can't imagine this day without them.

Asher smiles at his grandpa, who beams back at him, their features matching, the two looking similar for only an instant.

It's perfect.

Everything is perfect.

He's perfect.

Luca leads me to the front of the standing crowd, my legs move without thought, the crowd falls away. Luca slips my palm into Asher's. His fingers wrap around mine, strong and warm and assuring.

Luca slips away to stand at Gabriel's side. At the head of the crowd, just before me stands... my mother. The breath is knocked out of my lungs and a gasp slips from my lips as my eyes lock onto the Infinity witch, her bare feet practically teetering on the edge of the rocky cliff before us.

Lines crease around her olive eyes as she smiles down at me, knowing exactly what I see. Today I'm doing something my mother never could; marrying the person I love. I bite my lip and look away, into the white clouds as tears sting my eyes. My chest aches as a shuddering breath fills me and I wipe quickly at the corners of my eyes.

Asher gives me a curious look but takes my hands in his again, giving me a half smile as he leans closer to me, pulling me toward him, his hands seemingly begging to hold me.

My eyes rake over his tall frame. His lips are set in this half-open smile like he isn't sure if he should celebrate yet. Like our fate might fall away from us again, tumbling over the cliff before we've even started.

His hair is combed, neatly parted but ruffled by the wind. He hasn't combed his hair in all the days that I've known him. It's different. It makes him look... responsible. Less like the reckless pike I gawked at through the compound window, not anything like the hybrid who stormed into this community, nothing like the hybrid who nearly died at my feet a year ago. He looks... confident and clean but also... like he can take care of me. Strong and strong-willed, but also calm and gentle.

He squeezes my hand. My eyes flutter down his crisp white button up shirt, he holds both of my hands lightly in his. My gaze scans over his clean black jeans, to his bare feet. His typical heavy boots are nowhere in sight.

Because we're going to jump soon.

My mouth goes dry and my eyes dart back up to his for reassurance. The sun illuminates us, shining brightly over us, his skin appearing paler against the light. My heart thrums against my chest, making me aware of its existence as it pounds loudly in my ears. I never really gave my heart much thought before I met him, but now it's like I'm alive just for him. He makes me aware of my own beating heart when I took it for granted every day of my life before him.

A smile passes from my mother to Jim as he fades the melody away, strumming the last few notes into the whipping wind. Tears run down Shae's face already. It's sweet but I can't help but wonder how lovely she'll find the ceremony when they start the rituals.

"Thank you all for joining us today," my mother says, a melancholy smile filling her delicate features. Her hair is pulled up high on her head, a white formal flowing dress falls to her ankles, a color that I can't remember her ever wearing before. Her voice is calm and endearing all at once and rattles my heart with thick, pent up emotions.

"We are all here this evening for the same cause. Because love found two people when they couldn't even find themselves." She pauses looking at us with more emotion in her eyes than I've ever seen.

"Love is the strongest emotion, stronger than man himself, stronger than envy, even stronger than hate. And that's the reason it has the ability to bring conflict and anger halting. It has the ability to tread over race and diversity and distance." She preaches to them—to us. Though she doesn't need to. Anyone who has ever felt love, really felt it, knows it's a conquering emotion. "The man and woman before us are an example of love. The two together symbolize an emotion so few of us are lucky to ever find and feel and experience."

The witch's voice cracks for just an instant and I'm firmly reminded she isn't my mother. But I get the feeling she, too, felt love rip away from her just as my mother had.

Asher's thumb brushes over my knuckles as he smiles down at me, he leans in, bringing his forehead to rest on mine, my eyes close gently. Our hands linger between us as we listen to the witch's smooth voice drift through our minds.

"The Gods created man but they didn't stop there. They blessed the fae and cursed the creatures of the night, oppressed the mortals and then the mystics. But what they didn't expect was the beautiful creation the vampires and mortals created themselves." I lift my lashes slowly to see Asher's face, his strong features set in hard lines, his eyes closed tightly as he listens to my mother's words. "They are unnatural, yes. But they are human, their hearts beat just as ours do. Asher's beats for Fallon's, just as her heart does for his. What the world doesn't acknowledge though, is that not everything beautiful is intentionally made and not everything intentionally made is beautiful."

Asher smirks at her words, his eyes lifting to meet mine. He traces my features, my mouth, with his eyes.

"We gather here as a group of people supporting the love that is this marriage, this *union.* Not between a mortal and a mystic but of two lives becoming one..." I lift my head glancing at my mother, who smiles knowingly back at me. "Kaino, if we could have the bondings please."

I watch quietly, my eyes scanning their movements as my heart makes itself known again. For a different reason though. The ritual is starting. I swallow hard, trying to force away the fear that is clawing at my dry throat.

Kaino joins the three of us at the cliff's edge, a thin twisting rope is held in one gloved hand. The witch takes mine and Asher's hands, lacing our fingers together before lowering our joined hands at our side. We stand side by side holding hands. It's a natural gesture but it now feels frightening and weighted. My nerves hum through my body as I wait to see what will happen next.

She takes the long rope in her bare hands. Her fingertips smoke lightly and a sizzling sound is heard. My eyes dart to her quickly but she doesn't expose any emotion. She holds a calm and blank stare.

As she leans into us, between our joined hands, the

rope held between the three of us, she whispers something. Her voice is low and barely audible.

"This is going to hurt. It had to be infused with magic as well as the dust of the Red Hills to mark him."

Asher's head turns hurriedly to me, his lips parted in shock but he says nothing. My spine stiffens at her words but I keep my composure as best I can.

My mother starts to chant a string of fast, rhythmic words that I don't understand as she laces the rope around our forearms, wrapping around us, tying us together, before crisscrossing the rope slowly down our arms. It burns like fire on contact and I wince, breathing hard through my teeth but no sound escapes my mouth.

La tull, La sol, es unte. Wil te rhoesa, wah unte.

La tull, la sol, es unte. Wil te rhoesa, wah unte.

La tull, la sol, es unte. Wil te rhoesa, wah unte.

Her words flow gently through my mind but don't hold any meaning. I don't know how many times she chants, how many times she crosses the flesh searing rope against our arms. My eyes clench tightly closed, and I breathe shakily through my nose.

I feel her at our wrists now, she unclasps our hands until our palms are flat against each other's palms before tying the rope around the back of our hands. I feel her knotting it there. My wrist hurts so bad I'm sure the flesh is gone entirely but I don't look.

She pulls our tied arms closer, my feet stumble against the smooth ground but Asher pulls at my waist, facing me to him. I open my eyes to him, we face each other, one step away from the edge of the cliff.

Our bonded hands fume white smoke between us, his face is stern but composed, like the pain isn't there at all.

"Breathe, Fallon. It's almost over," he whispers into my hair as he presses a slow kiss to my temple.

I do as he says and focus on my unsteady breaths.

"The two of you are now eternally bound."

I chance a glance toward Luca who nods for me to finish the ritual.

To jump.

My eyes dart nervously to the crowd who waits for me to plummet to my death with happy smiles on their faces.

"You know I'd never let you jump, Fallon," he says pulling me against his strong chest.

"You wouldn't?" I ask, hope fluttering through the thick cloud of panic in my lungs.

"Of course not," he says pressing his lips softly to mine, washing away all the fear in my mind. I meld into him, the pain in my arm barely surfacing with his mouth against mine. "I'd never put that much pressure on you," he says, his breath fanning over my parted lips.

His words are said strangely and confusion joins my overcrowded emotions.

But only for a moment.

He pulls me even closer to his body, wrapping his free arm tightly around my hip, my hand grips his shoulder out of reflex. My nails sink into his shirt as he leaps over the edge of the world.

The wind tears at our bodies and clothes, wrapping the layers of my dress around my legs as we fall toward the reaching waves below. I feel it the moment we leave the shielding magic that surrounds the Wanderer's world, like a bubble reluctantly popping all around us.

I clench my eyes closed and hide my head in his chest.

What if we're not a true match? Or worse, what if we are but I flounder in the water until I pull us both down to the dark ocean floor.

Our bodies hit the water hard, knocking the thoughts from my mind and the breath from my lungs, leaving me no further time to dwell on my fears.

The water's cool and is a relief to my throbbing arm, which now moves freely at my side, unbound as if the salt water dissolved the rope. Instinctively I cling to Asher. But it occurs to me I really will just drag him down. I unclench my fists from his shirt, my arms and legs fling rapidly through the heavy water. I push panic into each movement of my thrashing limbs. I am alone, drifting through the open ocean. An offering to the water fae in hopes that they won't kill me before I kill myself with my inability to find the surface.

I keep my eyes closed tightly, the pressure of my lungs press against the walls of my chest as I fight to find oxygen again.

Something brushes my leg, clasping around my ankle.

I scream, a muted and diluted sound of my fear. My legs kick strongly, trying to get away as I suck in small amounts of water in my irrational attempt to flee. The salt burns my nose and lungs and I almost want to cry, just add my pain and salt to the water that has taken me in as one of its own.

My body goes still, my mind wonders how I even got here.

I proposed to Asher. I proposed a life of love and freedom and commitment but I found death instead.

Would I reach the deep ocean floor before death settles in? I hope not. I hope whatever has its hold on me takes me away and devours me quickly.

My mind feels heavy and tired.

Just as my limbs relax around me, a strong, hard body pulls me against them. My head settles against their chest.

Asher.

The sound of his heart pounds wildly beneath me.

Luca was right.

He'd never let me fall.

TWENTY
SOMETHING ALMOST NORMAL

THE FIRE that was in my arm just moments ago has shifted to my lungs as I cough up salty water and choke for air. Asher lies me against the smooth, warm rocks of the shore, the waves drift in like a blanket over my toes and ankles. My hands clutch my throat as I lie coughing and shuddering for air that is slowly making its way into my pained lungs.

A seagull sits a few feet away tilting its head to the side, trying to understand why the human girl can't succeed with the basic task of breathing.

As I sit up, Asher kneels at my side, his hand resting flat against my spine, rubbing short circles between my shoulder blades. The tattered pieces of my dress cling around my ankles...probably what I thought was attacking me in the ocean...

He's entirely unaffected, like our cliff diving experience was just light exercise to him. His wet hair sticks to his forehead, brushing his eyebrows that are set in concern. Water clings to his long lashes as he watches me, waiting like the seagull for the human girl to catch her breath.

In a light zig zag pattern, he runs his finger down my arm. Water droplets cling to my flesh, my eyes trail his movement against my skin where he traces against stark black lines. A thin rope design is etched into my skin, crisscrossing down my forearm and wrapping around my wrist and the back of my hand.

I trace the lines as well, trailing behind his finger. A matching brand mars his forearm with the same intricate black lines. My heart warms and flutters at the sight of his branding next to mine. It's pretty in a strange way. Meaningful and touching. A memory I will never forget, nor will the lines embedded into my flesh allow me to.

"Are you okay?"

His voice is quiet. The world around us is alive and loud and we're just here, dropped into it, keeping to ourselves the best we can to not disturb the sound of the crashing waves or the squawking birds or the rushing wind. The sun set sometime between leaping from the cliff and nearly dying beneath the waves but the sky is on fire with an ethereal orange and pink glow, highlighting the heavens around us.

"Yes," I say, my breathing as normal as my tight bodice will allow.

His hand, lined in black, brushes my wet matted hair from my face. His thumb trails my jaw as he watches me in silence for a few minutes. "You let go," he says, a statement filled with thought and concern. "Months ago, I was afraid I'd never find you again and I had that same fear just now. I'll never let you go, Fallon, but that means nothing if you won't hang on."

"I-" I pause as guilt shakes into my chest. A chill runs down my spine and I fold my arms over my chest to keep some warmth in me. "I didn't want to drag you down. I don't want to drag you down, Asher. I'm not as strong as you are, I'm human."

His brows pull together as he tilts his head to meet my downcast eyes. "I'm human, too... Partly. I'm definitely not perfect and I am very much aware that you are not perfect, either."

"Thanks," I say sarcastically.

He laughs, his fingers digging into my thick hair as he tilts my head up. His beautiful eyes bore into mine. "I meant that we have flaws. I know you have flaws, but they are my own now. You are a part of me." He glances at his inky arm. "I wouldn't have dove into that water with you if I didn't think I couldn't take care of you. I'll always take care of you, Fallon. But you have to let me. We're a team, remember?"

I shudder at his words and the cool wind. *He wants to take care of me.*

"I'm sorry," I say, looking away, keeping my focus on the flat gray rocks.

"Don't be sorry." He pulls my body into his side. "We should go before we both freeze out here."

"Go where?" I ask glancing back up at the intimidating cliff high above us.

The jagged bluff is painted in a swirl of ominous black, white and red colors. The lines bend and arch together making a symbol of an eye. Its pupil is red but streaks of white burst from the center, seemingly seeing all. It's eerie and unsettling. A chill traces like a spider down my spine.

"It's The Eye of the Ocean." Asher's explanation doesn't seem to settle my nerves. "Some say it's a symbol of the watchful Capitol just across these waters. Some say it's a symbol of the hidden community of mystics."

"What do you think it is?"

A pause settles between us before he glances up at the ominous painting.

"Perhaps it's just a reminder that there's a higher power watching over us."

For whatever reason his description of The Eye of the Ocean sends a shiver across my flesh and my attention lingers on the strange image for several moments.

Taking my hand in his, Asher leads me up the rocky shore, the smooth stones warming my careful steps. He pulls me closer to his side, his previously pressed button-up is now sopping wet and clings to his skin, emphasizing the lines of muscle beneath. I pause as we stand at the bottom of a smoothly carved lane that trails up the side of the cliff, right next to the tumbling ocean.

"Has this always been here?" My feet pad quietly

against the flawless granite as he leads me up the strange path.

"I made it last night." He glances down at me as I raise my brows at him. "I wanted to make you a present for our wedding day. I stayed up all night."

"Why?" I can't help the smile that pulls at my lips.

Several hundred feet in the air we stop just outside a... house carved into the cliff. Two shiny windows look out at the ocean and a single stone hinged door is outlined in the center.

"Because I wanted something almost normal for us. I wanted to make a home for you, Fallon."

My heart's gone. I know it's gone because it's melted in my chest. I part my lips with a breath of air that's clouding my lungs as I stare up at his sweet gray eyes.

Pulling me against his side once more he opens the door to our home.

I've never had a home before...

I follow close behind him into a single room. Our single room that my amazing husband built for me with his bare hands on the night before our wedding. My body feels crowded with emotions, bursting with happiness and sentiments.

Strands of my messy hair cling to my face as I take in the dimly lit room. A dainty table with two wooden chairs fills the majority of the space, what appears to be a sink divots the counter on the right side and a bed barely big enough for just Asher fills the left side.

It's small and rough around the edges but it's mine.

It's ours. Asher made us a home, something I never even thought I wanted until this moment.

I bury my face in his wet chest, wrapping my arms tightly around his waist as I take a shaky breath.

"Do you like it?" he asks against my hair, sweeping his arms around me as hesitation and worry tread his voice.

I nod, not looking up at him as tears threaten my eyes. Asher loves me, he wants to take care of me, and he built me a house. The life I had, the future my government promised me, it wasn't this. It wasn't even close to the heart-pounding happiness that fills me now. How did I ever think I'd be content in that life?

"Are you okay?" he asks in a soothing voice, running his hand up and down my spine.

"I love you, Asher," I say, his chest muffling my voice.

His hands halt against my body, his muscles strung tight against me. I take a deep breath, knowing it's the first time I've said it to him and remembering how he ran away after saying it to me. I raise my head and look him in the eye, needing to know how he feels.

The arrogant and easy demeanor he normally possesses isn't anywhere to be seen. He takes heavy breaths as he studies my face.

Is he still worried he'll ruin my life?

Angling his head low he lingers above me. "I love you, too," he says, his breath fanning my lips just before he presses a kiss hard against my mouth.

A kiss like I've never felt before passes between us, a

feeling of urgency fills my nerves as our bodies rush to close the space between us. I fist his drenched shirt in my hands, wrinkling it even more. His palms travel low against my back, past my waist, cupping me to him before grasping the underside of my legs, my damp dress tangling in his fingers as he lifts me from the ground. My thighs lock around his trim waist instantly, finding alluring warmth everywhere our bodies touch.

With fluid composure he carries me to our bed, skewing the neatly made blankets as he pushes me up the mattress with just his hips. He holds his weight above me on his forearm as his other hand runs down my side sending shivers over my cold body and grips my hip.

My heart pounds faster with every flick of his tongue and I find myself rubbing against his lean hips to release the energy that's building low in my stomach.

A groan passes over Asher's soft lips, an encouraging sound that has me rocking my hips harder against his, my breaths faltering with every torturous move he makes.

I'm not filled with nervousness like I thought I would be. He sets the pace and all I can think about is how amazing his hands feel against my damp skin.

He tears his lips from mine as he presses sweet and delicious kisses across my collar bone, slowing us down ever so slightly. I arch my neck to him, my back bowing into his chest, my brows creasing in pain and pleasure as his hand trails down the side of my dress and settles between my legs.

Just as my eyes widen, my breath scraping against my

lips with the feel of his meticulous fingers, it occurs to me —far, far back in my foggy mind—that this delicate and complexly laced dress will need to be taken off. The thought vanishes as his pace quickens, a moan escapes me just before he seals his mouth to mine and rips my virtuous white dress up the side in one quick move; saving us both a lot of time and trouble.

"What do you think will happen to us?" I ask him in the darkness, just as my mind begins to settle, the furling energy within me calming finally.

He holds me against him, the bed is small, almost intentionally small. We have no choice but to wrap ourselves around each other. His hand makes leisurely work of trailing up and down my ribs at an irresistibly slow pace. Soft kisses feather over the curve of my neck, waking me once more.

"We'll live happily ever after?" I can hear the smirk in his voice, lightening the mood with his words, the tingling kisses starting up once more. Part of me knows it's a distraction tactic, he's trying to distract me from my thoughts, maybe he's trying to distract himself as well.

It doesn't work though, my mind is trailing over all that has happened this week, the good and the bad.

"It just feels like a waste now. We gave my camp hope. Hope we could have spread to other villages with their help. Now what? We go back and tell them we've been attacked. That the government doesn't like us nearly as much as our lord thought they did?"

A soft kiss is pressed to my temple, making me close my eyes and just enjoy the way his love feels.

It feels like... warmth and safety and... happiness fluttering through me on a whirlwind of feelings.

"I think we should contact your father," he says, his voice a ghost of a whisper.

My spine straightens, my muscles no longer relaxed beneath his calming touch.

"You know about that?" A cracking sound fills my nervous tone.

"I—I didn't follow you. That would be... weird. I just overheard you."

"From over a mile away?" I ask, a small smile tilting my lips.

"I can't reduce my impeccable hearing, baby." He dips his head into the crook of my neck again, making me shift restlessly against his hard body.

"You didn't go out of your way to focus on our conversation?"

Silence fills his response for a moment as he takes a deep breath, breathing me in, his breath skimming over my flesh, making me squirm in his arms.

"I think tomorrow we should gather a few close friends and make an undisclosed trip to the Capitol. Your father obviously cares for you, Fallon. Ayden obviously cares for you. You have friends in high places. We need to take advantage of those friendships."

With every breath, his smooth, bare chest moves casually against my shoulder blades, a minor movement but I realize my own breaths are now matching his. I relax a little in his strong arms, the swift movements of his palm resume up and down my side, lulling comfort into me with every sweep of his fingers against my skin. I close my tired eyes once more.

Asher's right. Tomorrow is a new day. With enough time we'll fix everything. Everything will be different tomorrow.

TWENTY-ONE
EMPTINESS

Asher

Restless fingers traced her beautifully jagged scar long into the night. Soft skin met my palms, trembling beneath my touch. I couldn't believe it was real. I couldn't believe she loved me, that she's my wife.

I fell asleep with that thought circling my tired but bliss-filled mind. It was the most peaceful sleep I've ever had, her light breathing and restless movements lulling me into quiet dreams.

Until now.

My frantic eyes search her out in the dark room, hands pushing at the covers to find her slim body that warmed my side during the night. But she's gone.

Shadows and silence are all that accompany me. I'm across the room and flinging open the heavy door in an instant. A muted sunrise greets my squinting gaze as I assess the miles and miles of blue crashing waves.

Panic floods me, clenching my lungs and crushing my chest with each passing second.

Something is wrong here. My human intuition mixed with my mystic heritage is enough for me to know immediately that something is very wrong.

Fallon wouldn't have left me.

Would she?

I tramp the illogical doubt down. My kind is a scar to this imperfect and disfigured world but Fallon has never seen me that way... Maybe in the beginning, at the compound but that was before... Before our lives tangled and twisted around each other, forcing us to see each other clearly.

Throwing on a clean shirt and jeans, I tug on my boots as I walk down the makeshift sidewalk to the shore.

I can smell her here. Against the salty smell of the sea is her calming scent.

What the hell was she doing?

Up the winding coastline, I follow her scent, the strong morning waves of the sea push against my footsteps, against the trail of her.

Why would she have walked the shore? Did she need space away from me? A breath of air from the cramped house I built her? Did she hate it?

I wish I knew where all the festering doubt is coming from. My instinct is to push it down and smother it out before it crawls deep in my mind. Harsh words of the world have always been thrown my way. This time it's different. This time I care what this human thinks of me. More than she will ever know.

Her scent fades in the breeze as the cliff that surrounds me ends and opens to the place that the Wanderers cast out their dead to the greeting ocean that will swallow them up—if the water fae don't get to them first.

I kick at the smooth rocks, trying to make sense of what the hell is happening.

Fallon wouldn't have left me.

She just wouldn't.

After all we've been through. After last night... She loves me.

Then why isn't she here?

I drop to my knee's as the strength to stand starts to become too much. Water trails up in smooth, lazy waves, lapping at my jeans and drenching my thighs in cold salty water. My eyes trace the surface of the sea and I find myself leaning toward it.

"Where is she?" I whisper to the ocean, knowing it can hear me.

My heart pounds a nervous beat. I know what I'm asking for. I'm disturbing a race that would murder me just for addressing them, but I don't care. I have to know if she's safe.

The waves begin to still, the body of water becomes motionless, and I lean into it a bit more, looking into the clear blue water.

A long mass of white movement slithers up the coast

just beneath the surface, rippling the stillness with every twist of its spin. The water fae slips through the ocean until it's in walking distance, it crawls up to me on spindling colorless limbs. Slick white flesh covers its bony body, from its thin, lengthy feet to its smooth hairless head. Blank orbs stare into my eyes, she's just inches from my face and studying me intently. Her lips part, each small tooth comes to a jagged point that she's raking her pale tongue across as she breathes me in. Slits at the side of her neck move rhythmically as she inhales and exhales.

"You dare to call on me?" she seethes in a scuttling whisper. Eerie, clear eyes narrow on me, pinning me to the sandy shore.

My hands drape lifelessly in my lap, my shoulders pulled low with vulnerability. I clench my jaw at the weakness that's slipping into my body as my heart thunders through my chest. "Where did she go?" I ask again in a hollow voice.

The water fae extends her willowy arm, running an eager and glossy wet finger over the black lines that now scar my forearm.

"We witnessed the offering yesterday. The two of you crashed into our world, wishing to find our blessings on your bonding."

I wouldn't have let these things take Fallon away. We jumped to make the Wanderers happy but if the water fae believe they're entitled to the woman I love they're in for a rude awakening.

"She flailed in the water like she might kill herself

without our help. She released your bonded hand the moment she was able to." I jerk my arm out of her clenching reach, her slender finger hanging hesitantly before she brings her hand back to her side.

"Where is she?" I ask again through clenched teeth.

The fae lifts her smooth face toward me, the sun drying her features as the waves continue caressing her legs and arms. Her boney spine twists, curving her body unnaturally as she looks at me with a playful smile.

"She left." A mysterious light flickers in the hollowness of her eyes as she points a lengthy finger in the direction I already know Fallon went. "A look of emptiness was all the girl possessed. Perhaps she escaped our ready claws yesterday but the girl has more demons than meets the eye."

A shaking breath slips through my tight lungs, my fists clenching at my sides, a battle of helplessness and anger fill my body. I stand from the water, staring down at the creature that kneels at my feet.

"Disrupt my morning again and I'll rip your pretty face from your chiseled jaw and eat it for breakfast, my darling." Giving me one more long stare she slips back into the calm waters, her body snaking into the waves as she swims toward whatever hell she resides in.

I race up the cove, running in a blur as fast as my feet will carry me. I need help and the only mystic that will help me is the only friend I've had since my brother died.

Gabriel's white eyes fall on me with a smile marring his smug face.

"I thought you'd hole up down there with you wife for weeks. Didn't expect to see you so soon."

He almost laughs but his face falls. Without even seeing me, he knows something isn't right.

"What's wrong?" he asks, rushing to my side.

I push my hand through my hair that still holds the smell of the sea we dove into yesterday. My breath is ragged, not because of the run, but because of fear. Fear of losing her. Again.

"She's gone. I—I don't know where but she's gone."

He grips my shoulder, grounding me with his worried and cryptic stare.

"Gone? You would have heard her if she left, Ash." He nods, trying to calm me with reason, but it doesn't help.

"I didn't hear anything. I slept with her in my arms. Not a sound was made but when I woke up this morning I was alone."

The word alone comes out as a broken and pitiful sound that makes me cringe.

"Hey, she didn't leave. She wouldn't have left you. Get rid of that thought. That isn't what happened, I'm sure of it."

Thousands of worse ideas come tumbling through my mind at the sound of his reassurance. If she didn't leave me then she's missing... She was taken...

"What's going on out here?" Luca emerges from our hut in one of Gabriel's shirts, hugging her arms around herself as she squints up at me. "Why are you here? Where's Fallon?"

I shake my head and keep shaking it for several moments. Fear wrecks my body, pressing in on me with nowhere to go and my breath comes out in a long and jagged heap. *Where is she?*

Luca's lips part, as her wide eyes search my face.

"Let me get dressed. We'll wake my father. It'll be okay, Asher."

I nod at her as I swallow hard, pushing down the climbing fear that's clawing up my tight throat.

Last night I told her I wanted to take care of her.

I couldn't even keep her safe for a day...

Anger replaces the dread that consumed my body just moments ago. The hybrid—the traitorous hybrid is hiding something. I didn't tell Fallon how much it felt like a set up when I was captured. How quickly Declan fled when the guards arrived. How little trust this hybrid holds in my eyes.

The six of us sit at the table just as the sun creeps over the horizon. An hour has been wasted making sure all the important parties are present.

An anxious beat pats against the dry dirt as my boot taps restlessly beneath the table.

Kaino's stern dark eyes hang on every word I speak, his

limited emotions cross his face in a look of worry. Lord Raske's features are set in edgy lines, Gabriel and Luca sit on either side of me. Luca's as afraid of losing her friend as much as I am. She hasn't stopped biting her nails since we sat down.

The only person who doesn't hold a look of fear or worry or even distress is Declan. The hybrid focuses on the deep etched lines of the heavy wooden table. His eyes dart back and forth against the polished surface as he taps his fingers repetitively against the table top.

"And you said you followed her scent up the coastline?" Lord Raske asks, tilting his head at me, interrupting my thoughts on the suspicious mystic across from me.

"It disappeared where the opening lays, the trail was swept away in the wind." I pause, the rest of my words falling away in thought. "What do you know?" I ask, my burning gaze settling once again on the hybrid.

His head darts up immediately, his wide eyes hold… regret in them, making them appear full of liquid steel.

"I—Nothing. I don't know anything." The look washes away, once again full of hidden secrets.

Why did Fallon trust him? He has mistrust written all over him.

"If you know something about where she is, if you consider yourself a friend—she was a friend to you." I can't even bring myself to finish a sentence. My fists clench tightly, my nails biting into my shaking hands.

Gabriel's blind eyes shoot toward Declan, seemingly trying to gauge his appearance, his demeanor.

"He's lying," Gabriel says, his unseeing gaze narrowing on Declan.

Raske and Kaino pin the hybrid with a tense stare, the father and son sharing a mirrored look as they watch him.

"I have no idea what happened. Perhaps she realized the mistake she made." Declan folds his hands neatly in front of him as he settles his sneering eyes on me.

My jaw tightens until it hurts, my teeth grinding together as I stare at the worthless hybrid across from me.

"You had better be careful. The only thing tying me to this community, to the mock kindness I've shown you, went missing this morning. Fallon was the only thing protecting you from me. I won't play nice without her."

He swallows visibly, studying me without fear.

"I'll find her by myself. Your help isn't needed." I push my chair back in a rush, not bothering to wait for Gabriel or Luca as I storm out of the tent.

"I know where she is."

His calm voice trails after me, stopping me dead in my tracks. My back tenses, the muscles there strung tight as I wait for Declan to explain. I can't look at him. I'll kill him if his words aren't meticulously careful.

"She went back to the Red Hills."

TWENTY-TWO
CRIMSON EYES

Asher

It takes everyone in the room to tear my furious hands away from his throat. He lies pathetically gasping on the floor, his chair knocked over to the ground as I struggle to push Gabriel, Raske, Kaino and Luca off of me.

"Why? Why did you take her there? Why did you take her to them? You knew they would captivate her!"

Sharp and angry questions flow through me one after the other but I already know the answers. Declan wants acceptance. He wants it as much as I want solitude. The vampires of the Red Hills accepted him. They told me so themselves. He was their pet.

And now Fallon is, too.

I thought they hadn't done it. I thought they had let her go, for whatever reason. That wasn't it at all, though. They just couldn't get through to her while she lived within the protected, spell shielded walls of the Wandering community.

A tremor shudders through my body as I think about what they might be doing to her.

I clench the hilt of the Crimson Sword at my waist, my hands shaking against the cool metal as I stalk from the room. With a leaping start I rush in the direction of the Red Hills without a backward glance.

It takes less than an hour for my anxious but relentless steps to carry me to the base of the Red Hills. The cursed, blood stained air filters through my lungs. I begin the hike up the mountains, my hurried steps faltering against the damp crevices. Gabriel joins me moments later, breathing hard from the run here. A minimal amount of stress is relieved just from his presence.

Until Declan climbs up a minute later.

I scatter down to his level, bringing rocks and debris with me as I land in front of him, my sword raised. My boots echo off the rocky terrane as I stomp toward the hybrid.

He holds his hands up quickly. "I want to help. I want to help her, I swear," Declan sputters.

Gabriel holds me back lightly, waiting to hear the traitorous hybrid's reply.

"I didn't know what they wanted with her. They said they wouldn't hurt her, that they needed a human to release them from the curse. The race that damned them would have to be the one to release them."

My lungs burn as I take deep breaths to force down the aggression that's rising in me.

"They won't hurt her. Just let me talk to them. They trust me," he adds as I just stare wildly at him.

This lowlife hybrid just ruined her life. I thought I would be the one to do that but she did. With the help of her friend.

I turn from him, sheathing the sword, knowing I shouldn't waste any more time. Gabriel lowers his arm from me and starts climbing. I raise one hand, prepared to begin the climb, as well, until I think better of it. Declan takes three steps forward before I clench my fist and slam him hard in the face. A pleasant and fulfilling cracking sound meets my ears. I release a long, pent-up sigh as a burst of dark blood flows from his nose and down his chin.

He clutches his broken nose that's unfortunately already healing.

Damn hybrid healing!

He stares at me, not with anger but understanding like he knows he deserved that and more. I release another long breath that shakes my chest, just wanting to be able to breathe again. I won't breathe with ease until she's in my arms again.

I turn from him, not feeling threatened in the slightest with my back to the hybrid. The three of us trail up the mountain side in silence.

When we're close to Pike's Peak my feet begin to

falter. *What if they took her? What if we're too late? What if she's dead?*

I swallow hard and pull the Crimson Sword from my belt, holding it tightly in my hand as I walk cautiously toward the vampire's lair.

I'm prepared to fight them. I'm prepared to die. I'm not prepared for the sight that greets me.

Blood coats the already dusty red mountains. My heart thrashes, trying to release the fear and anxiety building within me. I don't want to see what's around the bend, where the vampires reside, starving and wasting away for the last several decades—just dying for fresh blood.

The sword clatters to the ground, greeting the cursed earth that it was wielded from. It's forgotten the moment I drop it, the moment my eyes land on her. I step over it, taking hesitant but eager steps toward the woman I love.

Within the shadows of the mountain she sits, shaded from the sun, her arms hanging at her sides with slouching and defeated posture. She's alone here. The heavy spell-bound boulders that sealed the vampires within Pike's Peak have been pushed away. Because Fallon freed them...

Shifting crimson eyes meet mine, a feeling of fire passes through my stinging heart. It stutters in my chest as I take in her altered appearance.

"I... I... I'm sorry," she says to us, her ruby like eyes sparkling with confusion and something similar to shame in the scorching sunlight.

With cautious steps I walk to her, my boots make no sound against the crumbling remains of the boulders that once shielded the world from the last remaining monsters. Blood smears her palms, like she fought to keep her mortality within her.

Kneeling before her, simple understanding lays heavily within me as I hold her gaze, my fingers cautiously trailing up the black lines that ink her cold wrist.

In this moment I am reminded of what I've always known: I know from too much experience that life can change in an instant, from one pounding heartbeat to the next… your life can crumble all around you. I know that there isn't a whole lot that an Infinity witch's dangerous magic can't fix. I know that my heart beats for Fallon Fiercely… I'll always love her.

Even if she is a vampire.

The End

The final book, *To Kill a Vampire* will be here on October 13! Reserve your copy today!

To Kill a Vampire

ALSO BY A.K. KOONCE

Paranormal Romance

The Cursed Kingdoms Series

The Cruel Fae King

The Cursed Fae King

The Crowned Fae Queen

Reverse Harem Books

The To Tame a Shifter Series

Taming

Claiming

Maiming

Sustaining

Reigning

The Villainous Wonderland Series

Into the Madness

Within the Wonder

Under the Lies

Origins of the Six

Academy of Six

Control of Five

Destruction of Two

Wrath of One

The Hopeless Series

Hopeless Magic

Hopeless Kingdom

Hopeless Realm

Hopeless Sacrifice

The Monsters and Miseries Series

Hellish Fae

Sinless Demons

The Secrets of Shifters Series

The Darkest Wolves

The Sweetest Lies

The Royal Harem Series

The Hundred Year Curse

The Curse of the Sea

The Legend of the Cursed Princess

The Severed Souls Series

Darkness Rising

Darkness Consuming

Darkness Colliding

The Huntress Series

An Assassin's Death

An Assassin's Deception

An Assassin's Destiny

Stand Alone Contemporary Romance

Hate Me Like You Do

ABOUT THE AUTHOR

A.K. Koonce is a mom by day and a fantasy and paranormal romance author by night. She keeps the fantastical stories in her mind on an endless loop, while she tries her best to focus on her actual life and not that of the spectacular but demanding fictional characters who always fill her thoughts.

Printed in Great Britain
by Amazon